Love And Work

A Valentine's Day Novel

By Dahlia Dempsey

📚 Other Books by Dahlia Dempsey 📚

Our Time
- 💕 Romance
- 👨‍👧 Single Dad + Single Mom
- 🍓 Slow burn
- 📚 forced proximity
- 🌶 spice
- 🚫 Forbidden Love
- 😛 Reversed age gap

Love and Work
- 💬 Rom Com
- 👫 Friends to Lovers
- 👨‍👩‍👧 Why Choose- at first
- 👫 Close Proximity
- 📚 Office Romance
- 🌶 SPICE spice baby
- 🐶 MFM

My Evil- Book 1
- 😈 Age Gap
- 🖤 He Falls First
- 🤫 Secrets
- 👫 Forced Proximity
- 🌶 Spice
- 💋 Opposite Attract
- 🔮 Twist Ending

Table of Contents

Chapter 1 Alice

Chapter 2 Alice

Chapter 3 Alice

Chapter 4 Logan

Chapter 5 Alice

Chapter 6 Logan

Chapter 7 Alice

Chapter 8 Logan

Chapter 9 Alice

Chapter 10 Logan

Chapter 11 Alice

Chapter 12 Logan

Chapter 13 Alice

Chapter 14 Ryder

Chapter 15 Alice

Chapter 16 Logan

Chapter 17 Alice

Chapter 18 Ryder

Chapter 19 Alice

Chapter 20 Logan

Chapter 21 Alice

Chapter 22 Alice

Chapter 23 Logan

Chapter 24 Alice

Chapter 25 Ryder

Chapter 26 Alice

Chapter 27 Alice

Epilogue - Alice

Epilogue - Ryder

Copyright © 2025 Dahlia Dempsey

All rights reserved.

This is a work of fiction. Similarities to real people, places, or events are entirely coincidental.

No part of this book may be reproduced, or stored in a retrieval system, or transformed in any way without the permission of the author.

First edition. January 10, 2025.

ISBN: 9798306017839

Written by Dahlia Dempsey

PA: Britney Oliver

CONTENT WARNING

This book is not suited for people under the age of 18 as it contains language, sexual encounters, and mature scenes.

Love and Work is a standalone with a duet coming soon.

Love and Work

Fan Art by Farida Hany

Love And Work

A Valentine's Day Novel

By Dahlia Dempsey

Dedication:

To my new PA, I couldn't have done it without you.

Chapter 1 Alice

"Why are all the good ones taken?" I ask my co-worker and best friend, or I should say my now ex co-worker, as I pack up the contents of my desk. She's still my best friend even if she keeps giving me hell over quitting.

"You always seem to pick the shitty guys, Alice," Becky lets slip out of her mouth.

Becky and I have been friends since day one at RedLights Co. We both got this job right after high school which was about four years ago. We started in the same week, so we were labeled "the new girls" from day one. Even after 4 years, people still call us the new girls.

With us both being administrative assistants for the two owners, our paths kept crossing. Eventually we just became best friends. Our company is the number one light producer in the state. I guess it's my old company now. We supply any kind of light you could think of. From kitchen oven lights all the way to the little lights your vibrator has. Let me just say, there have been some interesting conversations I've had to be a part of. I won't say I'll miss those awkward moments, but I'll desperately miss Becks.

"So it's my fault Noah was a jackass?" I ask with a tilt of my hip.

"No, but it is your fault for not listening to me when I told you not to get involved with the boss's son," she says with a pointed finger.

How was I supposed to know that Mr. Connor's son was a pathological liar and the worst human ever made? It doesn't help that it skipped a generation. Mr. Connor has always been the nicest boss I've ever had, but I cannot work with Noah any longer. I can't stand to see his smug face day in and day out.

He is the COO of the company, so he isn't going anywhere. Mr. Connor has apologized profusely. I'm assuming he is trying to avoid a sexual harassment lawsuit, but that's not me. I'd never do that. I'm a grown adult. I consented to several nights of mediocre sex. Apparently Noah has a hard time keeping his dick out of his co-workers. Something I wish I had known before spreading my legs for him.

"I know. You were right. You have no idea how much I wish I had listened to you," I admit to Becky. I'm seriously hating the thought of having to find another job and make new work friends. Thankfully Becks has a friend in a manufacturing business close by. They are looking for a new AA, but I still have to apply. Plus, the interview isn't for another week. I'm not sure what I'm going to do with my time until then. Maybe this will be the excuse I need to give my apartment a good spring cleaning, even though it's January.

"At least if you get this job, you will be close and we can meet for lunch regularly," she says with a hopeful smile.

"I sure hope so, but I'm trying not to get my hopes up too high. I'm sure there are several people applying for that job," I say with a frown. I can't help but be excited at the thought of a fresh start. Though I hate leaving Becks, I need a fresh start. This is the only job I've ever had outside of student worker jobs in college. I need to see what else is out there.

"You're going to get it. Everyone loves you, Alice. It's impossible not to. You have this energy about you that makes everyone either fall in love with you or want to be you." I can't help but smile at Beck's declaration.

"So which one are you?" She looks at me puzzledly.

"In love with me or wanting to be me?" I playfully ask. My shoulder is met with a hard slap.

"You're funny, but you already know I'm secretly in love with you and hoping and praying that you come over to my team," she toys. Becks is definitely a lover of females, but she doesn't like to label herself. She's proud of who she is, but she also doesn't believe it's anyone else's business. I've aways admired her for that "I know who I am and don't give a fuck if you like it or not" attitude.

"Oh I know. If I ever do start swinging that way, you will be my first call," I joke with her. We both know the other is playing around, but secretly we both know it's the truth. If I ever wanted to test those waters, Becks would be the one I went to because I wholeheartedly trust her.

With a smile, Becks gives me a wink and grabs one of my boxes and follows me to the elevator. It's just past 5 o'clock on a Friday night in Oklahoma City, so the streets are extremely busy once we make our way out of the building.

Heading straight for the parking garage, we toss my boxes into my car and say our goodbyes. I wipe a tear that's forming in my eye. "Stop it. It's not like we're moving far away. We just won't be working together anymore. We will still be at each other's apartments all the time. You know I can't stand Jarid and his obnoxious girlfriend. Even though I catch her staring at me," Becks says in one breath as she raises an eyebrow at the last part.

I can't help but laugh. How am I going to bare working without her? "Alright, alright. You're right. I need to suck it up and stop being such a crybaby," I say, shaking off the chill that just ran down my spine. It's freezing out here.

"There you go. Now get your cute butt in the car, and I'll see you soon." Becks slaps my butt just as I'm turning towards my car.

"Thanks, Becks. I'll see you soon." I start my car and watch as she jumps into her truck that's parked right beside me. I sure hope she's right. I sure hope we don't lose touch. I hate when people say they will keep in touch but don't.

I sit at the bar ready to puke. After three days of wallowing in my own sadness, Becks told me she couldn't watch this anymore. Her roommate, Jarid, told Becks his good friend, Logan, was single, so here I am. I told Becks no a thousand times. Apparently my caving point is one thousand and one.

Looking at my watch it's already 8:32 p.m. We were supposed to meet at 8:30 p.m. Sure he's only two minutes late, but what if he is standing me up? It's Thursday night, and I've already had two guys come up to me asking if they can buy me a drink. I'm not going to lie. I was tempted to say yes to that last one.

I have my interview tomorrow with Russell Colbren. He is the CFO at BigBockCox. Becks send me information on the company. Apparently they make mechanical devices for toys. "So I'm going to work at Santa's toy shop?" I asked while she helped me get ready for my date tonight, which got me an eyeroll.

With the help of Becks, I'm dressed in tight high waisted jeans that have large rips in the knees. They don't provide much warmth, but they sure are cute. The top I picked out is an oversized cropped knitted sweater. It comes about an inch above the jeans, so I'm dressed comfy but cute. I struggled with the shoes though. Finally landing on a black pair of low cut boots, I give myself a smile in the mirror. Becks curled my hair after I put on my regularly low key makeup. I've never been good at being a girl, but tonight I feel pretty.

Checking my watch again, it shows 8:39 p.m. Seriously? I could have gotten that hot guy's number and let him buy me a drink, but instead I told I was waiting on someone. He quickly moved on to the girl at the high top table by the bathroom. I guess he wasn't too broken up about it since his tongue is now down her throat. Wow. That took ten minutes.

"Are you Alice?" I hear a deep voice from beside me. Dragging my eyes off the newly joined couple, I'm met with the lightest green shade of eyes I've ever seen. They are almost a pale green, and paired with his light brown hair, they pop even more. Scanning his face, I linger on his chiseled jawline and sexy stubble. I've always been a sucker for stubble. Like why wouldn't you keep facial hair if you were a guy? Facial hair can turn a boy into a man in two seconds.

I shake my thoughts out of my head and reach my hand out. Trying to seem unbothered by this man's raw beauty, I say, "Yes. You must be Logan." He takes my hand and slowly shakes it, only he doesn't let it go. "I am. I apologize I'm late. I was getting you this." He pulls out a single pink rose. I'm not sure where he was hiding that, but I'm suddenly intrigued. I see him give himself a quick glance in the mirror behind the bar. Vain much?

"Where were you hiding that at?" I ask as I peer around him. His hand is still grasping my hand. I can't help but be annoyed by him. Don't get me wrong, he is hot as hell and I wouldn't turn around if I saw him naked, but he is one of those smug guys that think he can get anyone off of his good looks. He's a player, and he sucks at hiding it.

I'm met with laughter. "That's not the reaction I was expecting," he says as he rubs the back of my hand with the rose. I guess that's my sign to take it.

"Does that line usually work for you?" I say as I take the rose out of his hand and roll it between my fingers. Thankfully, there are no thorns to avoid, which I'm assuming he bought it that way.

"What line?" He asks with a shocked look. I may be judging him pretty quickly, but I can read him like a book.

"It's fine. I'm honestly curious if it typically works?" He laughs a little as he bows his head. When his eyes meet mine again, they seem friendlier. Almost as if he is seeing me in a different light.

"Are you always this suspicious of your dates?" He gives me the most innocent look. As if he is offended by my accusation.

"Only the cocky ones," I retort, shrugging my shoulders. When I do I remember our hands are still joined. Why won't he let go? "Can I have my hand ba-," he interrupts me before I can finish.

"Cocky? You think I'm cocky? Me?" He asks with a chuckle.

"Let's see, you arrive late, instead of checking me out you were checking yourself out, and you assume a flower would excuse you for being late. I'd say, yes. Cocky." He scans me with questioning eyes.

"I'd say you're ballsy and it's hot." That comment alone proves my point.

"Can I have my hand back?" He looks down at our joined hands.

"But they look so good together, don't they?" He runs a finger over my hand, and I hate to admit that it sends a shiver down my spine. Thankfully, he doesn't notice.

Ignoring him I ask, "You didn't answer my question." He looks at me with those beautiful green eyes. "Which question was that? I seem to have lost focus." He continues his teasing on my hand. It shouldn't be sexual. It shouldn't have my full attention. Our hands are still in a handshake for crying out loud, but I'd be lying if I said my stomach wasn't doing flips at his touch.

Doing my best to ignore his forwardness, I say, "Does that line actually work on women?" His laugh is immediate. I take advantage of his surprise and pull my hand out of his. Swinging my chair back towards the bar, I take a drink of my rosé that I ordered trying to calm my nerves. The nerves are still there, but not the same as before he arrived.

I can't decide if I'm attracted to this guy or not? Sure he is the definition of hot with his shaggy brown hair that is reserved for surfer boys, and his beautiful jawline. But he is aggravating. He oozes cocky, and I am not into that. "I'd say it works 99% of the time." He admits with a half smile.

"I'm sorry to have ruined your perfect streak." I say with a shrug.

"I'm sure you can make it up to me somehow." He raises an eyebrow at me and winks. A shiver goes right to my neck. I don't know why, but a hot guy winking at me is a huge turn on. Damn it, why can't I like you? Smirking, I ignore his sexual innuendo.

My attention goes to the couple in the high top table. The one with the hot guy that tried to buy me a drink. They are still making out. His hand is under the table, sliding under her skirt.

Just think, that could have been you, Alice.

Most people can't see it, but the way she is sitting, it's right in my line of vision. I can feel my cheeks start to flush as he teases her inner thigh. The last person to have their hand under my skirt was Noah. He convinced me to screw in the supply closet last month. While it was thrilling, it wasn't great for me. He hardly ever took his time with me. I'm not sure why I kept going back to him. Maybe it was out of convenience, but he rarely got me off.

I squeeze my legs together with the ache growing between my thighs. It's been a month without sex, and I am losing it. My vibrator can only do so much. I was all set to take this blind date home if things went well, but there is no way in hell I'll be taking Logan home. He would annoy the shit out of me before he stepped into my room.

"So, you like to watch?" I hear Logan whisper in my ear. He is much closer now than he was a moment ago. How long was I watching them for? It only felt like a few seconds. When I whip my head towards him, I'm met with heated eyes. He's only two inches from my face. Somehow his chair is now touching my chair. His arm is butted up against mine. How did I miss him moving? Was I that distracted?

"What? What are you talking about?" I ask, playing qoy. He leans a little closer and points his finger to the couple I was just watching. As he does this his fingers graze over my arm. I follow where his finger points, playing dumb.

"You were watching that girl about to get finger banged. No shame in that. I like watching too." He gives me a dark smirk.

He thinks he has figured me out. He thinks he is about to get lucky. Sure, I was watching them. Sure, I was turned on. Hell, I'm still turned on, but it has nothing to do with Logan. I give him an evil grin as I'm hit with an idea.

"Oh do you? You know, that guy hit on me just before you got here. That could've been me getting finger banged under the table," I say as I move myself closer to him. My lips graze his ear and my hand glides over his thigh. Drawing circles on his leg, I slowly inch up with every pass. "Just imagine, you could be watching me with my legs spread wide as a stranger sinks his fingers deep inside me."

I look down to see his dick growing. Satisfied with my evil plan I say, "Too bad you'll never get that chance." I hop off the stool, toss a $10 bill on the bar and grab my purse.

Logan's jaw is hanging open as I ready myself to leave. "Let's pretend we had a nice date but it's just not a love match. It was nice meeting you, Logan. I hope you have a fun night," I say as I toss my long blond hair over my shoulder and exit the bar.

Chapter 2 Alice

"How did the interview go?" Becks yells into the phone. I just got out a few minutes ago, and I actually think they liked me. The CFO was pretty funny, and his assistant was sweet. It was nice to be able to joke during an interview. From the moment I walked in, he put me at ease. It definitely helped that he was tall, dark, and handsome. I can't say I'd complain seeing him everyday. Although, he may be distracting. He dripped with confidence. Every move he made was effortless. Even when he cleared his throat. That rumble he made. "Hello?" Becks interrupts my daydream. I seriously need some good sex.

"Oh, sorry. It went well, I think I actually have a shot at getting the job." I tell her. Though it would be great to be the CFO's assistant and see his sexy face everyday, it's probably best that the position is for the COO's assistant in the production house. I didn't get to take a tour today as they are having their inspections today, but he told me they make a variety of items. He was a little vague, but I couldn't care less what they made. I just want the job.

"I knew they would love you. I told you!" She says with a loud excited voice. "Now tell me how your date went? Jarid is dying to know." I went to sleep before she had asked about it last night.

"Oh it was interesting, but definitely not a love match. Thanks for trying," I tell her. I hear her annoyed sign on the other end of the phone.

"I didn't set you up for a love match. I set you up for a good screw. Jarid showed me a picture of Logan. Even I think he is hot. Why didn't you just take him home and use him for the night? We both know you could use it," Becks admits. Yeah, she is definitely right. I could use that, but not with Logan.

"Honestly, he was annoying. I wouldn't be able to enjoy myself with him. The only way I couldn't have taken him to bed is if he didn't talk."

"Then why didn't you tell him to shut up and to put his mouth to better use?" Becks asks. She does have a good point there.

Images of Logan's face between my legs flood my mind. I feel my core clench. Why didn't I think of that?

"He was too cocky. You know I'm not into pretty boys that know they're pretty," I say as I pull into my apartment complex.

"Well you need to find someone to have fun with. You don't need a love match. You need a human pleasure toy. You and I both know there are plenty of men that would love to be that for you. You're hot." I smile at Beck's words.

"Thanks Becks. Love you. I'll see you tomorrow for drinks?"

"Absolutely. Wear something slutty. Maybe we can both get lucky tomorrow," she says as she hangs up the phone.

I promised her I'd go out with her to the local lesbian bar. I doubt I'll be finding someone to take home, but I can be a great wing woman.

"What about her?" I ask Becks as I nod to the cute redhead in the corner booth. She is clearly shy and with friends. Becks like the shy ones. She says they are usually the freakiest in bed.

"She's cute. Now if only I could find someone to distract the guy she is with," she says, giving me pouty eyes.

"How am I supposed to distract a gay guy? With these?" I grab my boobs that pour out of my tight black crop top. The three buttons at the top, only for show.

"Hey, even gay guys like boobs. I'm sure you will think of something." She bats her eyes at me this time. "Please."

"Let's get this over with," I say as I down the rest of my drink. Becks claps her hands together like a little girl.

We walk over to the corner booth as we pretend to be lost in a stimulating conversation. Once we reach our destination, Becks smiles at the cute girl with a pixie cut. "Do you mind if we join you?" Becks asks, sliding into the booth before she can answer.

"Of course," pixie says with an adorable smile. I wonder if Becks is right about this girl? Is she a freak in the sheets?

My focus goes to the guy sitting across from pixie and Becks. His face is hard to read. He doesn't seem very welcoming. You'd think he would slide over so I could sit by him, but he doesn't make a move. The only movement that happens are his eyes drifting to my boobs. I guess Becks was right about even gay guys liking tits.

"Do you mind if I sit?" I finally ask, realizing he is not going to offer. His eyes drag back up to my eyes.

"Sure," is all he says, but he still makes no move to scoot over. I look at him with a confused look, but instead of playing his game, I pretend like it doesn't bother me. Maybe he is waiting on his boyfriend to return and doesn't really want me to sit down.

"Ryder, be nice," Pixie says. With a smile, he scoots over one inch. I'm not even exaggerating. He moves over one inch. With a scoff, I slide in. Every part of me is touching him, but I pretend not to care. I also pretend not to feel his gaze burning a hole into my skin.

When I look over, he has a scowl on his face, and he is staring me down. What is this guy's problem?

"Can I help you?" I want to escape his gaze, but I can't. I promised Becks I'd help her tonight.

"What are your intentions with my sister?" He asks just as Becks and Pixie walk off to the dance floor. His eyes never leave mine. The vein in his neck throbs as he watches me. Now that I'm up close, I see how attractive he is. His dark hair is buzzed cut, allowing a great view of his deep blue eyes. His jaw is covered with the sexiest scruff.

"Your sister?" I blink for a moment. I never would have guessed that was his sister. They look nothing alike. "I have zero intentions with her." I point a hand over to Becks and pixie.

"Which one of these girls has your eye?" His face softens just a little. I wonder why he is so worried about his sister?

I can't help but let out a laugh. "None of them."

"Are you that picky? There has to be at least one girl in here that is your type." He scans the bar. "What about that one? She's hot." He nods over towards the girl watching me. She is tall, with long dark hair. Her skin is a few shades lighter than me. She is stunning I must admit.

"I'm not into girls. I'm here with my best friend," I say pointing towards Becks. Surprise sparkles in his eyes. "Are you here to chaperone your sister? Not really your scene either, is it? I think there is a male bar around the corner." I see the change in his demeanor before I hear him bust out laughing.

"I'm not gay. I can't say I've never thought about trying dick, but I like pussy for sure." As soon as he says that, I slap a hand over my mouth. I can't believe I just assumed he was gay. I'm mortified.

"Oh my gosh. I'm so sorry. I just assumed you were one of those very hot manly gay guys," I say before I realize I just called him hot.

"You think I'm hot?" A sly smile skims over his face. There really isn't any reason to be coy about it.

Obviously he is hot, but I'm not sure he knows it. Maybe he does, but he hides it better than Logan did.

"Have you looked at you?" I just go with it. I've had a few drinks tonight, and my filter is long gone.

"No, but I have looked at you," says as he places his arm around me and pulls me impossibly closer to him. I wait for him to say something else like "you're hot" or "you're beautiful" like most guys would say. Only, he doesn't.

His eyes roam down to my neck, down to my boobs where they linger there for several minutes. My breathing becomes more ragged the longer he watches. My chest is visibly raising and falling much faster than it was, and I can't help but pull my legs together. His eyes drop down to my thighs at the movement.

"I can help you with that, if you want," he says nonchalantly, nodding down to my thighs. The way he says it, it's almost as if he is genuinely being nice. He only wants to help me out and not simply get his. He acts as if I said no, it wouldn't make a difference to him. Like saying you want coke at a restaurant but they only have pepsi.

"Help me with what exactly?" I ask. I think I know what he is referring to, but what if I'm mistaken. It's hard to read this man.

"That aching between your thighs. I can tell by the way you're pulling your legs together that you need a release. I can give that to you, if you want." Once again, his words are dull. He could have just asked me about the weather.

My nerves get the best of me, "I have to use the restroom." I walk towards the bathrooms without looking back. To my surprise, there isn't a line. There is always a line. As soon as I open the door, I'm even more surprised. It's only a one stall bathroom. Why would they have that? Maybe there are more than one set of bathrooms in this place.

Just as I'm about to shut the door, a firm hand pushes the door open. Just as I'm about to scream, he turns the lights on and shuts the door. It's Ryder. "What the hell are you doing?" I'm shocked, but I don't feel worried. I don't get that fight or flight feeling with him.

"Wasn't that code for "follow me to the restroom"?" He looks at me with questioning eyes. Before I can answer he locks the door and starts walking towards me. "Do you want me to leave? Say the word and I'll walk out that door." His forward steps don't stop until he reaches me. My feet instinctively step backwards until my back is pressed against the wall. I'm pinned between him and the concrete wall.

My heart is racing so fast I'm worried it's going to pop out of my chest. This can't be normal. This can't be okay. I must be going into cardiac arrest. "Just breathe. I'm just here to help you. I don't want anything in return. I simply want to watch you come apart at my hands."

Am I hearing this correctly? Is this really happening? This stranger wants to give me an orgasm with nothing in return? That's hard to believe.

As if he can read my thoughts, he tucks a strand of my hair behind my ear and says, "You're too beautiful to be in such great need. I could see it from the moment you slid in next to me. I'm going to get you off. Then, I'm going to leave."

I hold my breath as he drags that hand that was once in my hair down to graze my nipple. I don't have a bra on so he can immediately see them harden. "Just watching you is satisfying enough."

I nod my head in agreement. Maybe I do want this. I've never done something so reckless in my life. It's not like I'm having sex with him in a bar bathroom. I'm just going to let him touch me.

He closes the distance. His lips are on mine and they are hungry. One hand fists into my hair. The other grabs my left boob. The sensation of his rough kiss and talented fingers makes a moan slip from my lips.

My hands grab the back of his neck and pull him harder against me. The weight of his body covers me in warmth, and I relish in it.

Lost in the moment, I tug at his hair. It earns me the most delicious moan, and I swallow the noise. "You definitely need a release now. Don't you?"

His heated eyes meet mine and all I can do is nod. His luscious lips curve into a smile. The hand that was on my boob drops down to my stomach, then my waist, then to the waistband of my jeans.

I suck in a deep breath as his experienced hands unbutton and unzip my jeans. Knowing what's about to come next, I instinctively pull my thighs together. I'm desperate for his touch. I'm desperate for a release.

I shamelessly grind on his hand as he cups me outside of my jeans. "I can feel your heat through your jeans. I can't wait to see how quickly I can make you cum. I bet it will be quick." His words drag out my wetness. I can feel it pooling at the bottom of my panties.

Without warning, he dives past my waistband and into my panties. With the first flick of his finger along my swollen nub, I shudder. He's right, it's not going to take long at all.

He rubs my clit back and forward, in circles, and up and down. With every new angle I grow closer and closer. With every movement of his fingers, I want that much more. I want to feel those fingers inside of me, but I don't want him to stop what he's doing.

I guess this man can read my body because he slowly inserts a finger into my channel, and I tighten around him. Then, two fingers are inside of me. He continues as he rubs me with his thumb while thrusting his fingers inside of me. "Oh god yes. Just like that."

My head has fallen back against the wall, and before I know what's happening, my orgasm rolls through me. The waves come in sharp bursts as he rides them with me. Slowing his pace of his fingers, he slowly pulls out of me. "Do you feel better?" I'm jello against the wall. All I can do is nod.

He smiles a hooded smile, buttons me back up, adjusts himself, gives me a once over, turns and walks out of the door.

Chapter 3 Alice

"This will be your desk. Mr. Miller's office is right behind you. He will be in later this morning. Grab some coffee and I'll take you to meet some of the co-workers. I'll let you know who you can count on and who you need to avoid," Sinclair says. She is Mr. Williams, the CFO's assistant.

"That sounds great. Thank you," I say as I set my purse and bag down on my new desk. It looks so fancy. It's much nicer than the one I had at RedLight Co. I can't help but smile.

I got the call about five days ago. They offered me the job just two days after I interviewed. Apparently Mr. Connor from RedLight Co. called in a great recommendation.

Five days ago I accepted this job. Six days ago I got finger banged in the bathroom of a gay bar by a ruggedly handsome straight man. I can still feel his fingers inside of me. I've been kicking myself all week for not getting his phone number. Those hands were too good not to experience again.

I sigh. He didn't even know my name, so there is no way he could get in touch with me. The only reason I knew his name was because his sister told him to be nice. Oh, was he ever nice to me.

Becks had wondered where I'd gone. When I told her what happened, she high-fived me and told me, "It's about damn time."

"Are you ready to meet the gang?" Sinclair asks, shaking me out of my thoughts. I quickly set my coffee down and look up at her. She's got to be close to six feet tall.

"Absolutely!" I follow her down the hall towards the production house. The engineers, IT guys, and pretty much all the fancy smart people are on this side of the building.

I run my hands down myself to smooth out the pencil skirt and white short sleeve blouse I picked out this morning. I feel a bundle of nerves gather as she leads me into a group of cubbies. "Everyone, this is Alice. She is Mr. Miller's new assistant. Be nice to her," she says loudly.

About eight heads pop out from behind their privacy walls. One set of eyes are familiar the moment they lock on me. "You have got to be kidding me," I say under my breath when Logan walks out from behind his cubby.

He is dressed in gray slacks that almost look like jeans. It's paired with a fitted red polo, and completed with white and red converse. I've never been a big fan of collared shirts, but I must say it looks pretty good on him.

"What are the odds, Alice? Did you come here just to watch me?" He questions with a smile. I'm assuming he is referring to the time he caught me watching a couple from the bar be intimate for a moment.

"Oh no. I only watch people I'm interested in," I say with a twist in my face.

"Do you two know each other?" Sinclair asks as she takes a step back.

"Only if you count being ditched at a bar," Logan spits out. I'm not sure what the company policy is on dating co-workers, but I really don't want to get written up on my first day. Not that it should matter. We didn't know we'd be working together.

"I did not ditch you. I simply got bored and left," I retort and immediately regret it, but thankfully, Sinclair starts laughing.

"You two are going to be some great entertainment." She rattles off everyone's name and job description as she goes down the line of cubbies. I forget them as soon as I hear them. I'm the worst with names.

"And you know Logan. He is our head of IT. If you have any issues with your computer or anything techie, ask him," she says with a nod.

"Nice to meet you all," I say towards everyone, but I purposely keep my eyes off Logan. I cannot believe he works here. I bet Becks knew that bit of information and decided not to include that. She knew there is no way I'd have gone on a date with him had I known.

"I have to get to a meeting. Get settled in your office. Logan will come by to set up your computer, phone, and login shortly, and I will swing by right before lunch." She turns on her heels before I can say anything.

My eyes glare at Logan right away. "Are you trying to get me fired already?"

"Why would I do that? Now I get to toy with you even more," he says with a playful wink. Damn him and his winking.

I take a step closer to him so I can whisper. I can feel eyes on us. "Stop. Oh my gosh. I don't want my boss knowing I went on a date with the nerdy IT guy." I put my hand on my hip.

He chuckles and takes another step closer to me. "Nerdy? I think you mean sexy IT guy."

"You do think highly of yourself, don't you?" I say with a platonic pat on his shoulder.

"Oh don't pretend you weren't thinking about how I'd look naked as soon as you saw me," he says with a smile. I'm glad he is joking and not being serious. Funny Logan is way better than cocky annoying Logan.

"How can you read my mind so well?"

"It's the face. It says it all." He gives me a shrug.

"Your face or mine?" I tease because he definitely has a nice face.

"That's a good question. Now I can't decide."

"Oh good lord, Logan. How am I going to get any work done with you around?"

"Too distracted already? It's okay. All the women have been there. Even some of the men have. I'll try to keep my distance when you have work to do," he winks at me again.

"You are so sweet to think of me in this hard time." I look around and notice everyone else has gone back to work. I guess no one notices us which is good.

"What can I say, I'm a nice guy. You really missed your chance, Alice." He blows me a kiss. "I'll be over in a bit to help you set up. Try not to get too nervous with anticipation."

Rolling my eyes, I walk back towards my desk. It's a straight shot down a long hallway. Once I get to my desk, I turn around because I feel eyes on me. Logan is watching me with the cutest smirk on his face. All I can do is shake my head.

Taking a seat at my desk, I fumble with my belongings and place some personal items on my desk. Looking up, I realize Logan has a straight view of my desk. Sitting in his chair, he is leaning back talking to someone on the phone watching me. Note to self, keep my legs closed.

Chapter 4 Logan

"She works here?" I ask into my receiver. I'm furious Jarid didn't tell me she was applying for the admin position. There is no way I would have gotten involved with her had I known. Not that we are involved. She left a few minutes into the date.

Shaking my head I think back to that date. I was shocked at how beautiful Alice was. With her long slightly curled blonde hair flowing over her shoulder, and her bright blue eyes, I was lost. But I didn't want her to see that, so I put up my cocky persona that always works when I'm picking up a girl. Only it backfired on me. I guess Alice isn't into cocky guys. She put me in the friend zone so fast, I got whiplash. Though I'm not a fan of the friend zone, I've never been friends with a girl I haven't slept with. It's probably best now that we work together.

I was kicking myself for being late. I'm never late to things. I really was getting her a rose for her, but that wasn't the real reason I was late. I noticed an elderly lady carrying four grocery bags up her stoop. She almost fell twice in the two minutes I was watching her. I couldn't in good conscience leave her there, so I grabbed her bags for her only to see she had another flight of stairs to go up. It took fifteen minutes to get up one flight while holding the bags and her hand. I told her it really wasn't safe for her to be going up and down stairs like this. Thankfully, she wasn't offended by my bluntness. She informed me her son usually does all the shopping, but he is down with the flu. It made me feel a little better after dropping her off at the top of the stairs.

"Yeah, and?" Jarid states.

"I can't date someone I'm working with, jackass."

"Is it against the company policy?" Technically we could date, we just can't date our superior.

"Who cares. You should have told me, dude."

"My bad man. I didn't see the issue. Did you see her? She's hot as fuck. I didn't think you would care if she eventually worked at your same company."

"Whatever man. You could have just told me and let me decide that."

"Yeah, you're right. Sorry dude." There is a long pause before he starts talking again. "But she's hot as fuck, right?" I can't help but laugh.

"Yeah. That she is. I got to go. See you later." Hanging up the phone, I steal a peak at Alice.

It's not enough that she works here, now I have to have a direct view of her all day long.

When she left me at the bar, I was so turned on. I had to basically run home and jerk off. I haven't been able to get her off my mind. The way she was so unphased by my appearance and douchebag persona. The way she spoke to me so seductively and just left. It's not the usual "I want to get in her pants" kind of situation. I mean, don't get me wrong. I'd love to get in her pants and watch those small perky tits bounce up and down as I slammed into her. Fuck. I look down and see my dick starting to get hard.

Alice is different. I think I could actually be friends with her. She catches me staring at her, so I play it cool and give her a nod. I guess now is as good a time as any to set up her computer.

Giving myself a few minutes to calm down, I make my way over to her. "Miss me already? You just can't stay away, huh?" She teases.

"I'm glad you saw right through me. I just can't stop thinking about you. I think I'm in love," I say with the most serious face as I lean down on her desk. Her once joking eyes turn serious. Is that fear in her eyes? I start laughing as I make my way around her desk and invade her personal space.

"Jeez. You're too easy. I'm just messing with you." Although, I did jerk off to her that first night. Things will be different now though. We clearly shouldn't be anything more than friends. Plus, I don't think she'd want to.

Pulling on the back of her chair, I ask, "Can I drive?"

"Can you drive what? How am I supposed to know if you can drive?" She gives me a weird and confused look. How cute. She has no idea what I'm talking about.

"I mean, can I sit there and mess with your computer?"

"Oh, why didn't you just say that?" She stands up and slides past me. Her ass grazes against my leg. Damn it. Think about puppies and kittens and that grandma you helped out the other day.

Thankfully, the grandma image worked. I take a deep breath and shrug it off and do my best to focus on her computer. Even if I'm not trying to date her, I'm still a red

48

blooded male. If a nice ass grazes close to my dick, it's going to react.

I spend the next few minutes setting her up with all the logins and granting her access to the company files. "Is this how you want your desk setup?" I question her. I'm half hoping she will want to move her desk over to the other wall so I don't have to see her all day long.

"Yes, this is fine. I don't think we should move it." I nod my head and get back to work. Plugging in her phone and adjusting her settings, I make sure everything is working properly.

She sits down on the desk right beside me. It takes everything I have not to look over at her long toned thighs that are only inches away. Her black pencil skirt hugs her perfectly. It's sexy without being unprofessional, and that blouse she has on. It's probably thinner than she realizes because everytime she pulls her arms back to stretch, I can see her hard nipples. I can't help myself from taking a peek as she does it again. I have got to stop looking at her.

Pushing the chair back, I crawl under her desk to hook up the last of the cords. Rolling onto my back to pull the printer cord down through the desk, I hook it up to the computer.

Just as I'm about to get up, I notice Alice watching me. Not only is she watching me, her eyes are glued to the lower part of my stomach where my briefs barely stick out of my pants. She is getting a good view of the V that disappears into my slacks. Enjoying the attention, I take longer than necessary to plug in the printer. I can't help but grin at her as I finally emerge from under the desk.

"Your equipment looks good," I mumble as I stare at her chest. She definitely heard me because her arms instinctively cross over her chest. If only she knew, that makes her tits perk up even more.

Unable to stop my smile, I brush off the invisible dust on my pants. I wipe off my crotch deliberately slow, and it works because her eyes drift down to me.

"Thanks." She says quietly which is unusual for her. "It's about time. Are you always rolling around on the floor like that for people? Or am I just special?" Her quick witted self is back.

"Don't you know by now," I pause for dramatic effect. "You're special." I give her a wink.

"Good thing you've realized that now. Or I'm not sure we could be friends."

"Is that what we are? Friends?"

"Other than the obvious."

"What's the obvious?" I question. Feeling the conversation go serious.

"That you're secretly pining for me." She lets a smile cover her face, and I can't help but smile right along with her.

"Oh that's right. I almost forgot about it. Thank you for reminding me. I'll go back to my stalking now." I give her a small push with my elbow.

"Can you let me know when you plan on sneaking into my bedroom? I'd like to make sure I have both my baseball bat and my make-up done."

The thought of sneaking into her bedroom has my mind wondering. "So, just friends?"

She puts her finger to her lips and taps as if she is thinking. "Yup. I've decided. We're going to be great friends."

"That could be fun too." I wiggle my eyebrows at her. She has gotten my dick hard several times. Although she wasn't trying for the most part, I'm 99% positive she tried to that night at the bar. She isn't completely innocent in this, but I think that's what's making our friendship so fun. I don't want to use this girl for one night and then move on. I'd like to keep her around. She's funny.

"If you're with me, you're always having fun. Haven't you figured that out yet?" She smiles back at me.

"I have," I say with zero humor.

"So, is everything finished? Or do you need to drive some more?"

"I'm finished. Let me know if you need help with anything. I'll be right over there," I say, pointing to my cubby, "watching you." I have to admit, that last joke sounded a little more ominous than funny.

"Alright stalker. Get out of my space so I can get some work done," she says with a shooing motion.

"So what you're saying is I'm distracting you," I wink at her again. "It's my looks, isn't it."

"Bye bye cocky Logan."

Walking back to my desk, I turn to look at her over my shoulder and wave. She simply takes a seat and rolls her eyes.

Alice seems to have hit her stride working here. I've never seen someone fit in as quickly as she has. Even Rob from accounting likes her, and he hates everyone. "She's a funny one," he said to me last week. I'm pretty sure that was the first time he has said a word to me, and I've been working here for five years.

It's been 2 weeks since Alice first started working here. We have actually become really close friends. We talk about everything, from the people we're dating or not dating, to the mold she found growing in her food container she left here. She tells me about her over-bearing mother that insists she needs to come home more often, and I tell her about my annoying neighbor that just bought a parrot. All throughout the night I hear, "Polly want a cracker." Why would you teach your parrot to say that?

"Are you thinking about that dumb parrot again?" Alice interrupts my thoughts as she sits on my desk.

"It only knows one sentence."

"Polly want a cracker?" Alice says before I can. Alright, maybe I've complained about it too much.

"Shut up," I say as I softly punch her in the leg. She is wearing a shorter skirt today. It's much shorter than she usually wears, but she is wearing tights under it. She looks hot as fuck in it. I've been having a hard time keeping my eyes off of her today.

My hand lingers on her thigh longer than it probably should. "Why are you wearing this skirt today? Do you have a date tonight?"

"Why would you assume I'm only wearing this skirt because I have a date later?" She questions.

"So he can slide his hands up your skirt with ease." I mimic my words and slide my hand up her thigh just enough to make a point. Her eyes go wide with surprise.

"Logan, stop it." She slaps my shoulder, but doesn't make a move to move my hand. "I still have tights on. These things can keep out anyone." Does she really think that's true? If a guy wants it bad enough, nothing is going to stop him. Especially not some stupid tights.

"You're so cute to actually think that these silly things would keep us out." With the hand that's on her thigh, I pinch the tights, pull up, and let them snap back into place.

"I'm just saying, they aren't easy access. If I was going for that, I wouldn't wear anything under this skirt." She sticks her tongue out at me.

"You have to make a guy work for it some. Don't make it too easy on him," I say with a serious look.

"Sometimes it is fun to make them work for it, but sometimes you just need it then and there. If I'm in that kind of mood, I don't want these things in the way." She slaps her thighs.

"I'd just rip them off of you, if I was trying to get in your pants." I admit because it's the truth. If I want in the moment and the only thing between me getting what I wanted, those tights would be shredded.

"Yeah, I can see you doing that. Not going to lie, that would be hot to have someone rip my tights off of me because they wanted me so badly. I can't say I've ever had that exact thing happen to me." She sticks her bottom lip out and pretends to pout.

"Just say the word, and they will be on the floor," I joke with her. If she asked me to screw her, I probably would. I mean she's hot, but it's different with her. I wouldn't be expecting her to come whining to me because I forgot to call her last night.

"I'll remember that." She smiles at me. "I guess I better go back to work. Try not to watch my ass so noticeably this time when I walk away." She deliberately sways her hips as she walks back to her desk.

"Not possible," I yell back at her. And it's the truth.

Chapter 5 Alice

"You seriously haven't seen *White Chicks*? That is my all time favorite movie." I say to Logan at lunch. We have been spending all our free time together at work. Once you're not trying to date him, he is actually a cool guy. Only on rare occasions does cocky Logan come out, and that is usually a job. I've come to realize, it's almost like a second personality he brings out for fun.

"Can't say that I have, or that I'm jumping at the thought of watching it."

"Take that back," I slap his arm as he munches on a carrot.

"You can't make me want to watch a movie."

"No, but I can make you come over tonight and watch it with me," I give him my best Alice smile. An Alice smile is over the top but impossible to resist. He always ends up giving in when I tilt my head and gives him my puppy dog eyes with the exaggerated smile.

"Oh no you don't. I'm supposed to meet the guys tonight." He shields his face from my Alice smile.

"Look at me," I try to pull down his hands and force him to look at my face.

"The guys will kill me. They need my good looks to attract the ladies. You know they can't resist them," he says through his hands. He definitely is right about that. I can't believe how many women from the office come over and hit on him throughout the day. I counted one day, and there were seven different women. Seven.

At first the women were annoyed with me. They thought I was going to swoop in and take the eligible Logan. Once they figured out we are just really good friends, they stopped giving me the death stare which was a relief.

I release his hands and pretend to go back to eating my sandwich, but as soon as he puts his hands down, he is greeted with the best Alice smile I could possibly give. "Damn it, Alice," Logan groans. "Do you know how long it's been?"

"Been for what?"

"Since I've had any kind of action."

"Why would I know that?" I roll my eyes.

"The last time I came close to getting any action was when we watched that couple at the bar and you slid your hand up my leg." The memory makes me smile. That was fun teasing him like that.

"Oh you poor thing. How will you ever survive?" I rub his back in a comforting way.

"I'm not going to."

"Your hand not cutting it anymore?"

"Hell no. You and I both know it's not the same." He has a point there. It's been almost two months for me, and it's been extremely difficult. I love my vibrator, but it's absolutely not the same.

"We can all go out after the Valentine's Day party tomorrow. I'll even help you find a hot chick to take home," I offer. He looks at me with suspicious eyes.

"Deal." We shake on it and sit in silence as we both finish our lunch.

"How old are you? I keep forgetting to ask," Logan says in between bites."

"I'm 25."

"Nice, me too."

"Really? For some reason, I thought you were younger than me. Oh yeah, that's probably because of how immature you are," I joke with him.

"Shut up. You love it. When did you turn 25?" I always hate telling people when my birthday is. They always tell me how sorry they are.

"It's on Christmas Eve."

"Wow," Logan says. I wait for the oh I'm so sorry that must be so difficult to share your birthday with Christmas but surprisingly he doesn't say that.

"I knew you were special." A huge smile covers my face. I'm pretty sure he's the first person that has turned my birthday into a positive thing.

"Was Logan Spencer just sweet to me?"

"Don't get used to it," he says, without looking at me even though he has finished his lunch.

"When is your birthday?"

"November 13th."

"Just barely older than me." He laughs. We talk about our families as more people trickle in for lunch.

⇛→

"How are you not laughing at this?" It's at the part where one of the guys just ran into the rolodex of pens and knocked them all down with his fake boobs when he was trying to check into the hotel.

"It's not that funny," he says as he takes a sip of his beer.

Jumping up, I imitate the scene. "Sorry, these are new," I say pointing to my boobs and laugh which makes Logan laugh.

"Well, it's funny when you do it. Your tits are cute and small. They wouldn't knock anything down."

"Hey," I say, throwing a pillow at him as I take a seat on the opposite side of the couch. "I happen to like my little boobs."

"Shit, so do I." I hear him say under his breath.

"I heard that," I say as I give him the devil stare.

"Don't give me that look. I'll throw this pillow right back at you. I'm not above hurting a girl."

I stick my foot right in his face. "You wouldn't hurt me."

He grabs my foot but doesn't let it go. "No, but I'd tickle you." He starts tickling my foot, and I squeal like a little girl. Thankfully, he stops, but he still doesn't let go of my foot. I'm laying on one side of the couch with my feet in his lap. It feels nice to have him here. It may be the wine talking, but my whole body is tingling as he massages my foot with his big hands.

"Don't be making those kinds of noises over there, woman." Woman? And what noises?

"What noises?" Did I make a noise and not realize it? What kind of noise was it? Shit, I hope it wasn't an embarrassing noise. I mean, we are friends, but I still don't want him to hear me fart or burp.

"Everytime I do this," he rolls his thumb up the arch of my foot, "you moan." And sure enough, I moan.

"I can't help it. It feels too good." I lean my head back and enjoy the feeling of his warm hands kneading my aching muscles. My other foot starts to fall off the couch, so I move it up on his lap. As soon as I do, I feel the hard length of him under his sweatpants. My eyes go wide, and I look right at him.

"I can't help it. You're over there moaning. Plus, that chick looks hot in that skirt," he nods towards the TV.

"Oh, it's the girl in the skirt, huh?" The wine must be getting to me because I have this huge urge to tease Logan. I'm dressed in a white crop top and a flannel button up over it. I paired it with some comfy black leggings.

"Yup. That and the fact that it's been over two months since I've got any action. I blame you for that now."

"Me?" I give him my most innocent look possible as I take off my flannel shirt and throw it at him.

"Alice. What are you doing?" He gives me a serious look, and from Logan, that's rare.

"I'm just getting comfortable. That's all." I don't expect Logan to make a move, but teasing him is half the fun. He gives me a look that says, "I don't believe you."

"Cross my heart," I continue. Then, I draw an X over my chest. His eyes follow the movement of my fingers, but when I drop my hand his eyes don't leave my chest. It probably doesn't help that I took my bra off as soon as I got home.

I pull my focus towards the TV. Pretending not to feel Logan's eyes burning into my side, I start to play with my hair. Twirling it around my fingers and pulling it down over my boobs. As I let my hair go, I graze my right nipple.

Logan growls. I don't think I've ever heard him make that noise before. I'm not going to lie, it was hot. "Stop it, Alice," he says as he grabs both my ankles and pulls me closer to him.

My butt is against his leg. My legs are over his lap, and my thighs can feel his hardness. I'm confused by this close proximity. Normally, I wouldn't see Logan as anything more than my hot friend I like to tease occasionally, but right now, this close up, he has taken my breath away.

He grabs my arms and pushes them to their side. "Behave, or I'll make you pay." I wonder if he is serious? If he got too turned on, would he make a move? "I'm serious, Alice," he continues as if reading my thoughts.

"Okay. Okay. I'll play nice." I put my hands in the air as if to show him I'm surrendering. I have a feeling Logan would be very good at teasing. So good that he'd probably win, but damn it it's fun to see Logan all riled up.

"Why do I not believe you?"

"Because you have trust issues, Logan. You really need to work on that. It's not pretty," I say as I go to stand up. Since my feet are on the other side of his lap, I slide my ass over his lap and get a good feel of his dick. Yup, it's still hard.

"Alice Mitchell. If you don't get your ass off my dick, I'm going to shove it inside of it." It's the first time he has ever been so forward about it.

"Someone needs to get laid and fast. You're too grouchy when you're having withdrawals," I say as I get up and go to the kitchen to fill my wine glass.

"I am in withdrawal. I was being too good of a friend to you, and this is how you treat me." He points to his crotch.

"Oh poor baby. Yes, I'm so terrible. I let you feel my ass and see my nipples. I'm such a bad friend." I roll my eyes.

"I never actually got to see your nipples, but go ahead. Take your shirt off. I'll watch." I don't say anything as I go back to the couch and take my seat on the opposite side of the couch. "Yeah, that's what I thought. Now sit over there and behave," he scolds me as if I'm his child.

Sticking my tongue out at him, I watch the rest of the movie in peace.

Chapter 6 Logan

I watched her out of the corner of my eye all night. After she slid her ass across my lap, I couldn't focus on anything else. Her smell of roses and apples, the feel of her smooth skin against mine, and her teasing smile had me gripping the arm rest. It took everything in my power not to make a move.

She's your friend, Logan. She's just your friend.

Though we have only been friends for less than a month, it seems like longer. We just connected. Things are easy with her. We don't have to think or worry about the other. We just are. She's like one of my guy friends, only better.

Our work Valentine's day party is tomorrow. The owner's birthday is on the 14th so Valentine's day is always a big deal here. He gives us that day off with pay, so we usually have the party the Friday before.

Alice promised she'd take me out tomorrow and be my wing woman. Whatever that is. She may think she's going to help me get laid, but all she's going to do is detour women from talking to me.

She's a smoke show. If a woman sees me with her, there is no way they are going to try to compete with her. I don't have the heart to tell her that though.

"I better head home before I fall asleep. This is the dumbest movie, Alice," I tell her as I crawl over to her and nuzzle into her neck.

I'm cuddling with her on the couch as she watches the rest of the movie. Surprisingly, she doesn't give me a normal smartass remark. She simply runs her fingers through my hair.

Yup, I'm about to fall asleep.

Unable to stop myself, I kiss the side of her neck. Images of me trailing kisses along her jaw and down her chest flood my mind.

Shifting behind her, I pull her back into my chest. She wiggles her ass into me, so I grab her hips to make her stop. "Alice, I warned you," I growl into her ear as I start to run my hand up and down the side of her body.

She feels soft and tight at the same time. Dragging my fingertips over her hip bone, I circle it. Continuing my journey, I run my fingers along the waistband of her yoga pants. It would be so easy to slip my fingers inside and feel her.

Forcing myself away from her waistband, I softly graze down the middle of her leg. From the top of her hip bone down to her mid thigh, I trace the V shape her legs make around her most private area.

She hasn't moved since I started my tease. I know it's affecting her because I'm about to drive myself crazy. I want her to break first.

Trying one last attempt to get a reaction out of her, I loop my arm around her stomach and pull her against my hardening dick. She instinctively grinds herself on me. "Logan," she whimpers. I can hear the need in her voice. Bingo. She's turned on, and it's time for me to leave before I pull all her clothes off.

"Good night, Alice. I'll see you tomorrow," I say in her ear just before I give it a playful bite.

Damn this hardware failure. Apparently there was a squirrel that got really hungry last night. I'm sure he was looking for a warm place for the night and wandered into my network box. Let's just say, it didn't end well for him or my computers. It cut the network cables for the entire floor.

Whatever asshat left the wires exposed needs to be fired. My day just got a lot harder and a lot more stressful.

I've been working on it all morning and it's still giving me hell. At this point I'm not sure my balls are still on the outside of my body. I'm pretty sure they have retreated, and I don't blame them. It's cold as fuck out here. The one good thing about it is I've hardly had time to think about last night with Alice. The way she felt under my touch. Her ass grinding into my dick as I teased her with my touch.

Fuck. Stop it.

I've been all over the building today making sure everyone's computer is back up and running. I purposely make Alice my last stop. It's not because I'm trying to avoid her, it's because I want to spend more time with her and rant about my day.

Everytime I pass her desk, she either sticks her tongue out at me or makes a silly face. It always ends up with me laughing and shaking my head as I pass by. "You look ridiculous," I mouth as I walk by. It's a lie because she always looks beautiful. I've come to realize, she could wear a paper sack and still be the prettiest girl in this office. I'm going to have my work cut out for me tonight. She's going to attract every guy in the bar.

Sure, she says tonight is about me finding a girl to take home, but I have a feeling she is going to find someone faster than I will. She's going to be a terrible wing woman.

Walking past Alice's office, I knock on Mr. Miller's door. "I'm sorry, Sir. Do you have an appointment? I don't see it on my calendar, and Mr. Miller is a very busy man," Alice says in her most professional, chipper voice, knowing fully that she can't view the calendar until I reboot her computer.

Grinning, I look into the glass door and see Mr. Miller shooting wads of crumpled up paper into his toy basketball hoop that's stuck to the wall. "He looks pretty free to me. Unless you count shooting hoops as busy?"

"I'm sure it's very important," she pretends to blow me off.

"He needs me, Alice. He can't do any work without me," I say as I twirl some wires around in my hand.

"Mister fix it."

"I can do it all. Remember that, Alice," I say with a wink as I walk into Mr. Miller's office.

"Logan, just the guy I wanted to see," Miller calls out. He's finally stopped shooting baskets. Now he is leaning back in this chair with his feet propped up on his desk. Sometimes I wonder what he does around her. I think his assistant always did most of his work, now that's Alice. No wonder she always seems busy.

Don't get me wrong, he's the nicest guy you will ever meet. Him and Mr. Williams would give you the shirt off their back. That literally happened last year at the Christmas party. Things got a little out of hand, and one of the girls spilt wine all over her cream colored dress. With no warning, Miller took off his button up shirt and gave her the shirt to go change into.

When she came out of the bathroom, it looked like she just hooked up with a very large man. I let a smile slip from my face at the thought. I wonder if anything wild will happen today? You'd think they would have rules since it's on company property, but Miller and Williams are both heavy drinkers. There is always booze at the party, and everyone is encouraged to partake. I've never not left that party drunk. Tonight will most likely be the same. Although, I'll need to pace myself since Alice and I plan on going out afterwards.

"At your service, Sir." He jumps out of his chair without me having to ask. With a few clicks and wire change, his computer comes back to life. "You're all good, Sir."

"Please, call me Miller." He tells me that almost everytime I talk with him. It's just a habit my parents beat into me. "Always be respectful to your elders. Ma'am and Sir," I can remember my parents sending me to my room if I forgot to say, "Yes, Sir."

I nod towards him, and give him my famous Logan Spencer smile as I walk out of his office. "My last victim," I say to Alice. She has been organizing her desk over and over today.

"Did you save the best for last? Or did you forget about me?"

"How could I ever forget about my favorite girl?" It's a joke, but it's actually true. She is my favorite girl. I don't have other friends that are girls, so this is new.

"Oh, don't play with my heart, Logan. I just can't take it," she places her right hand to her heart and the back of her left hand goes to her forehead. She's so dramatic. I love it.

"You're too much." I shake my head as I round her desk.

"You ready to drive? Hop on." She pats her lap as if to signal me to sit on her lap. Yeah, that's not happening.

"If anyone is sitting on someone's lap it's going to be you."

"I don't think your poor head could take it." She winks, and I don't miss the double meaning.

"My head is just fine, no thanks to you."

"Your hand again?" She scrunches up her face and gives me a pathetic look like she feels sorry for me. "That must be rough."

Shaking my head, I'm at a loss for words for once. Usually I can go toe to toe with anyone, but this girl is my match.

"Cat got your tongue?" She sticks her tongue out. Only this time it moves from side to side.

"No, but it will tonight." Her mouth falls open slightly. Before she can say anything dirty back I motion for her to stand up. Thankfully, she does without a word.

The last few hours of my day are much less eventful, thank God. Everyone has started decorating for the Valentine's Day party. My eyes go wide when I see them bring in the kissing booth from last year. It was a big hit with most, but I will admit, it was pretty gross kissing some of these people. I'm still shocked they allow this at work, but Miller and Williams have never been your normal bosses.

"What the hell is that?" I hear Alice ask one of the ladies from HR.

"I don't see anything. I do not come to these parties or I'd have to fire everyone," Lana says as she covers her eyes and walks away.

Watching Alice approach me, she asks me the same thing. "Yo, Spencer. What's the deal with that thing?" We have recently started this new thing where we call each other by our last names.

"Oh, you're in for a real surprise, Mitchell."

Chapter 7 Alice

Never would I have thought a company party would be like this. There's a ton of alcohol from wine coolers to hard liquor. Most people brought a change of clothes, and I will say, some people are dressed very inappropriately in valentines outfits. "Who knew Beverley from accounting had boobs like that?" I elbow Logan in the side.

"I did," he admits with a laugh.

"You and her?" I feel my eyes go wide. I'm met with a hearty chuckle that I'm surprised comes from Logan.

"Hell no. She wears something like that every year." He gestures towards her outfit. "Don't get jealous on me now, Mitchell."

"Funny."

I see a woman I don't recognize stumbling over herself with a drink in her hand. One of the guys from Logan's IT team grabs her waist and slides his hand over her ass. "Are they together?" I point towards them.

He shakes his head. "No, but anytime they drink together, they end up doing more than work."

"You really weren't lying. This party is crazy for a work party. I feel like I'm watching the Christmas episode of *The Office*." Logan nods in agreement and smiles at me. We both love that show. It's almost a competition to see who can say, "That's what she said," the most. I like to think I'm winning, but it's probably pretty close to a tie.

"Told you. You will never go to a work party like the ones Miller and Williams throw."

Just as he finishes his thought, two guys from the warehouse bring out the booth. Finally I'm going to get to see what they do with this. Surely it can't be as innocent as a photo booth.

"You ready for this?" He asks as if this is really going to be a huge spectacle.

"You have got to be hyping this up way more than it is," I say out loud but more to myself than anyone.

"Everyone gather around," Sinclair clinks her glass with a small fork. "Girls, please come to the left side of me. Guys to the right." Everyone starts going to their designated sides. Everyone but me. I'm watching the crowd part like a sea of fish. They all know what's about to happen, but I don't. I can't help but be a little nervous.

"Don't chicken out on me now, Mitchell," Logan whispers into my ear as he walks to the right side of Sinclair.

Doing something my mother told me never to do, I follow the crowd. Standing on the left side of Sinclair, I listen intently as she explains what's about to happen.

"As most of you know, it's time to play *Kiss or Drink*." My face pales as I look over at Logan who is beaming. Am I going to have to kiss someone? And if I don't want to, am I going to be forced to drink? I've already had too many of Sinclair's famous mixed drinks. She wouldn't tell me what was in them. I feel my nose going numb already. Plus, I'm still supposed to go out with Logan tonight. I can't do that if I'm shitfaced.

"I have placed all the ladies' names into the bucket. Gentleman, you will draw out one name, but don't tell anyone." She places a finger over her lips. "When it's the woman's turn, she will be asked *Kiss or Drink?* She has to decide before she sees who drew her name. After that, I think it's pretty self explanatory. If she chooses *kiss*, she will go into the booth and her partner will come in after her. If she chooses *drink*, she will take two shots of her partner's choosing. Are we ready to play?" Everyone cheers and raises their glasses.

So, I'm going to have to kiss someone in this room. The last person I kissed was Ryder. Damn it that was a good kiss. The way he wanted to give me pleasure with nothing in return. I've never known a guy to be like that. Most guys are worried about their pleasure first, or at least getting theirs eventually. I've never had a guy only want to pleasure me to help me out then leave. I really wish I would have got his number before he left, but I was too high from my mind blowing orgasm to ask.

Focusing back on the game, I look over at Logan. "Here we go." He mouths to me and gives me a wink.

I watch as each guy grabs a name out of the bucket. When it gets to Logan, he quickly picks and reads his name. When his eyes look up, they meet mine. A grin covers his face, but it's quickly covered with a grossed face. I'm guessing whoever he got does not appeal to him.

Miller and Williams don't participate as they feel it would be unprofessional. I laughed as soon as I heard that. This is where they draw the line. That's good to know I won't have to worry about having to kiss the boss.

That leaves us with 11 women and 12 men. Sinclair graciously volunteered to go twice. Lucky for her, most of the men in the office are good looking.

When we get to the married women, they always look at their husbands before deciding. Most of them surprisingly choose *kiss.* There is no way I'd be okay with my husband kissing another woman, even if it was just for fun.

My turn finally comes about halfway through the game. I look at the five guys I possibly will have to kiss. Maybe I should be safe and choose *drink.* I know, it would be lame if I did that, but I really don't want to be kissing these guys I work with. I guess I can just give a quick kiss like most of the girls have done.

"Alice, it's time for you to choose, *Kiss or Drink,*" Sinclair says as if I'm on a reality dating show and I'm down to my final rose. I give Logan a questioning look and he mouths, "Just do it."

"Kiss," I say, but it sounds more like a question.

"Good for you, Alice. Please, make your way into the booth. Your partner will be there shortly.

I nod towards Sinclair and make my way towards the Booth that is in the middle of the two groups. Looking at Logan before I step in, I give him a funny face that says," *wish me luck".*

Stepping inside of the booth, I note there is no seat. Definitely not a photo booth then. It's just a box with a curtain similar to a photo booth. My nerves are getting the better of me. I can hear Sinclair talking. "Gentleman, who is the lucky guy that gets to kiss our newest member?" I hear clapping and then footsteps.

This is it. There is no going back now. Work is going to be so awkward Monday morning. Why didn't I pick *drink*? I stumble on my own feet as I'm trying to shift around in the box. Oh yeah, that's why I didn't pick *drink*. I'm already tipsy.

This box is tight for just one person. This is going to be a tight squeeze. I'm about to have my body pressed up against someone I work with. I'm going to have to look at them every day and know I kissed them. I shouldn't do this. Just as I'm about to bolt, Logan steps in.

"Logan?" I immediately relax. Oh thank God. It's just Logan. He smiles and steps all the way into the booth. His chest is completely flush against mine. I can feel his breath against my face as he starts to lean down. His right hand goes to my waist and grips hard. His left hand goes to my chin. Tilting my chin up with it, he whispers against me. "You ready?" It's the most serious I've ever seen him. Gone is the joking cocky Logan. The Logan that's left in his place is sweet and calm.

"For what?" The words finally leave my lips. I can't take my eyes off of his lips. I've never seen them this close up before. Even the day at the bar, I was looking towards the side of his face.

He ignores my question and starts to lean in. Oh my gosh, I forgot. I still have to kiss someone, and that someone is Logan. He is millimeters away from my lips now. Is it just me or is he moving incredibly slow as if not to spook me.

How am I supposed to kiss him? How does he like it? Why do I care? And what the hell do I do with my hands? I can feel myself freaking out, but the moment his lips touch mine I feel every muscle relax.

It's a gentle kiss. My hands are still at my side because apparently I've forgotten how to kiss someone. I mean, how do you kiss the guy that has become your best friend?

I feel his tongue brush against my bottom lip, and I'm in shock. I don't open my mouth to invite him in, but I do lean in against this kiss. Our lips start moving faster as my hands remember how to work. They dive into his beautifully full, chocolate, brown hair.

Our kiss morphs into an open mouth kiss, but our tongues never meet. I can feel myself getting hot, and that familiar buzz down between my legs. Feeling the need to break free of the kiss, I place my hands on his chest. With one gentle push, we break apart.

His chest is heaving. His eyes are burning into mine. His lips are puffy from our kiss. "What was that?" Logan finally speaks, but it doesn't sound like my Logan. His voice is deep and husky.

"I think we might be a little tipsy," I say as I start laughing. Bending at the knee, I rest my hands against the top of my legs. As soon as I do this, I get a great view of Logan's hardened length.

"I guess I'm going to need a minute," he says without shame.

"They are waiting on us out there. They are going to think we are still making out in here."

"We weren't making out. You wouldn't even use your tongue," Logan says as he dives into his pants and adjusts himself.

"Hey, that took me by surprise. I didn't know you were planning on doing that."

"I didn't know I needed to announce myself." He rolls his eyes.

"Okay, I'm getting out of here before they come looking for us. You good down there?" I nod towards his crotch.

"You mean, is my dick still hard?" I roll my eyes at him. "I'm good now."

"Well that didn't last very long," I snicker at him.

"You better get your ass out of this booth before I show you how long I can last." My eyes go wide. There is no humor in his voice. Damn. Serious Logan is hot, but also a little scary.

Without another word, I step outside of the booth. Everyone starts clapping, and I am completely mortified.

Chapter 8 Logan

"You're really going to wear that dress out tonight?" I look at her and bite my tongue. She's dressed in a red, skin tight dress that stops midway down her thighs. The neckline doesn't even exist in the middle. It has a huge deep V. The end goes just above her belly button.

"Fuck," I let slip out. Grabbing my forehead and massaging my temples as if I all of a sudden got a headache. She looks too good to go out with. All the guys are going to be hitting on her, and all the girls are going to stay away from her. Plus, I'm going to have a hard time taking my eyes off of her.

That kiss got me good. I honestly thought of us as just friends. Sure, it's fun to flirt with her, but I wasn't thinking of trying to start anything with her. Now, all I'm thinking about is her soft lips on mine. I didn't even get to feel her tongue, and I can't stop thinking about doing it again.

I really need to get laid.

"Yeah, why? What's wrong with it?" She asks nervously.

"Absolutely nothing. It's fucking gorgeous, and you look fire in it," I admit as I eye her up and down.

"Then why can't I wear it?"

"I never said you couldn't wear it. I'd never tell you what to wear, Alice." I'm serious when I say this.

"Okay. Then tell me what's the matter with it, Logan Spencer. Tell me why you asked if this dress was the dress I was going to wear out." Her voice goes up at the end signaling her annoyance.

"Fuck, Alice. It's because you look too damn good in it. No girl is going to want to compete with you. If you go out in that dress, I'll never find a girl to take home," I finally admit to her. I immediately feel bad because she turns and walks back into her bedroom. I'm tempted to follow her, but she shuts her door.

Damn it. I guess I screwed up this night. Why didn't I just keep my mouth shut.

Exactly three minutes later she exits her bedroom wearing ripped leggings and an oversized sweatshirt. She has taken most of her makeup off and has pulled her hair up into a bun. Great. She's not going now. Did I seriously make her that mad?

"Alice, come on now. I'm sorry. I wasn't trying to be a dick."

"I know," she gives me a big smile. "Let's go."

"Go? Go where?" There is no way she is still wanting to go to the bar, right?"

"To the bar to find you a woman. Come on. Get your head in the game. Spencer." I can't hide my laughter.

"You're going to the bar dressed like that?" I question her.

"You said no girl would come up to you if I dressed the other way, so here I am. Why is this so difficult for you to follow? Just get your ass in the car," she ushers me toward the door.

As soon as we make our way downstairs, the Uber driver is waiting for us. I watch as Alice hops into the car. Even dressed like she is, she's still the most beautiful woman I've ever seen.

"I can't believe you're really dressed like this for me," I admit to her. Most girls wouldn't be caught dead at a bar in baggy clothing.

"I promised you. A deal is a deal." She shrugs her shoulders like it's not a big deal.

She pulls her legs up into the seat and sits criss-crossed. Her knee lays over my thigh. Without thinking, my hand goes to her knee down her thigh and back up again. Her head leans over onto my shoulder. "Are you tired?"

"No, you're just comfortable," she admits without pulling her head up.

Arriving at the bar, it's already after 11. The work party went just past 9 before people started leaving. I had three guys come up to me asking how my kiss was with Alice. They all were jealous it was me that got to kiss her. I tried to play it off like it wasn't a big deal. We're just friends.

If I'm being honest, it was the best kiss I've ever had. I can't imagine how good it would be if I got to use my tongue. It would probably be too good. Even now I'm having a hard time looking at her as just a friend.

"Alright, let's go find you a woman." She jumps out of the car right after me. Pulling me with her hand in mine, we make our way inside. She drops my hand as soon as we get inside. "Don't want people getting the wrong idea," she gives me a wink.

Yeah, that would be just awful.

Alice leads the way to the bar and orders us two beers from the male bartender. He gives her a wink and retrieves the cold beers.

And so it begins.

I watch as every guy in this bar gives Alice a once over. She doesn't even seem to notice which blows my mind. How could she not notice every eye on her. "She is cute. Do you want to go over there?" Alice points to a cute blonde at a middle table with two other girls.

"How is this supposed to work? I've never had a wing woman."

"Easy, I'll go over and talk up my best friend. When they see how cute and funny you are, I'll step aside."

"Lead the way. I'll be right behind you," I tell her.

I watch as she makes her way over to the girls. Immediately they scoot over and let her sit down. Of course they like her, everyone likes her.

I watch for a few minutes as she talks me up to them. I don't need a wing woman or a wing man. I don't struggle with picking up women, but Alice seemed so excited to help me find one. Does she really care if I screw one of these girls?

"Alice, there you are. I thought I had lost you. I didn't realize you found us such great company," I wink at the blonde as I pull out cocky Logan.

"Hey, come on. Sit down," she gestures for the blonde to scoot over, and she does.

I focus most of my attention on the blonde as Alice talks with her two new friends. Maybe a wing woman is nice. She can distract the friends so I can focus on the main course. The only issue is…I keep watching Alice's lips.

They are still a light shade of red from her earlier outfit. A few pieces of her hair have started to fall out of her messy bun. They cascade around her face like a waterfall, and I feel like a complete idiot for thinking like this. She is literally serving me sex on a platter. But what if it was sex with her? No, there is no way she would ever be into that, and I'm not going to be the one to bring it up.

Before my dick starts to get hard thinking about having sex with Alice, I drag my focus back to the blonde.

"Would you like my number?" She fiddles with her phone as if she is nervous.

"Why wouldn't I? Have you seen yourself?" She giggles and hands me her phone. I quickly type in my number and hit save. "Send me a text so I have your number." She nods her head and sends it right away.

Someone is eager.

Maybe she is going through a dry spell like I am.

"Are you two really just friends?" She asks, nodding over towards Alice. I can't hide my smile because I'm asking myself the same question.

"We are." I don't feel like giving her more of an explanation, but I'm sure it won't stop there.

"Why haven't you ever dated? She's beautiful." Yeah, thanks for reminding me. Not wanting to answer her question, I decide Alice can.

"Alice!" I yell over the music. She lifts her eyebrows in acknowledgment. "She wants to know why we've never dated."

Alice giggles and waves a hand to the blonde, whose name I have already forgotten. "Because I'm a lesbian," she says and I choke on my beer.

"Are you okay?" The blonde pats my back as I nod.

"It went down the wrong way."

"Oh I hate when that happens," she says, and for some reason I don't think she's referring to a drink going down the wrong way.

I can't believe Alice just said that. That's one way to get these girls to relax, but what if one of them made a move on her? What would she do?

Damn it, now I'm thinking about her and one of these girls, or all of these girls. Fuck.

"I need a drink," I say as I go to stand up. I'm pretty sure the blonde next to me caught a glimpse of my semi hard dick.

Damn you Alice.

"I'll come with you," Alice says, jumping up. I ignore her, but she follows me anyway. "Was that girl rubbing your dick under the table?" Is she jealous?

"Why do you ask?" She laughs and points to my dick.

"Because you have a semi."

"Well you're the one that started talking about being a lesbian. It got me thinking about girl on girl action. Plus, that blonde is all over me."

"I guess that's a good thing. Let's get some shots for everyone." Alice jumps up to the bar and orders everyone two shots each. She is already stumbling a little. This may send her little body over the edge.

"Are you sure you need two more shots? And a beer?" I ask when I see she orders another beer for the two of us.

"It's Friday night. You're about to get some, and I'm a new lesbian," she says as she downs one of the shots. Great. Yup, she's officially drunk.

"Did you just say you're a new lesbian?" A guy behind her says.

"Um, I'm pretending to be a lesbian to help my friend get it in with that blonde girl over there," she nodes in her direction.

"Wow. You're a really good friend. I like your sweatshirt by the way. I think I have one just like it." This asshat grabs her waist as she trips over her shoe string. "You okay?"

"I'm good. It's these damn shoes." The guy heads her over to the nearest barstool and sits her up against it.

"I got you," he says as he runs his hands down the side of her legs. Extremely unnecessary to tie her shoes.

Fucker.

"If you like this outfit on me, you should have seen the dress I was going to wear."

"Is that so? Maybe you can show it to me later." He leans in to kiss her, but I stop him.

"Let's go," I grab her arm and start leading her outside. The guy she was talking to grabs my other arm to stop me.

"Dude, she wants to stay. Let her go." He tries to push me off of Alice as he grabs her arm. That was a mistake.

Getting up in his face, I never let go of Alice. "If you touch her one more time, I will knock every last one of those pearly whites out. You got it?" I tower over the guy by several inches. He may be buff, but I could still lay his ass out with ease.

"Whatever, dude. You're fucking crazy." He starts to back away.

"Come on, Alice." She huffs as I drag her outside.

"Why are we leaving? You forgot your blonde girlfriend. We should go back for her." Alice tries to walk back inside.

"It's fine. I have her number. I'll meet up with her later," I say, trying to get her to not think about the dumb blonde that I have no intention of meeting up with later.

"Oh that's good. I bet she can suck dick really well. She had a really big mouth." I can't help but laugh at her.

Once the Uber comes, we climb into the back of the car.

"You smell so good, Logan. Do you always smell this good? Why haven't I noticed that before? Did you just shower?" I laugh at her again.

Yup, one shot too many.

Pulling up to her apartment, I walk her inside. As soon as we make it into her door, she starts shedding her clothing. "It's so hot in here. Did you turn the heat up before we left?" Her sweatshirt hits the floor. Thankfully, she has one of her famous crop tops on.

"Let's get you to bed, Alice," I say as I usher her to her bedroom.

"Oh yes, let's get you into bed too." She swirls around and grabs at my shirt. Trying to pull it over my head, I grab both her wrists and pull them behind her back.

"Be good and get into bed. Stop trying to take my clothes off." Even though I would love to get naked with her.

"Party pooper." She gives me a pout as I release her and starts pulling the rest of her clothes off. Her crop top goes first. Once she pulls it over her head, she tosses it into my face like she did last night. Then, she fumbles with her leggings. Almost falling over, I move her back towards the bed.

"Sit down," I tell her firmly as I start taking her shoes off. Once they are both free, I stand back up to help her slide up into bed. Grabbing my neck, she pulls me down on top of her.

"Why don't you stay and cuddle with me? Your hands feel so good on me."

"Alice, stop." I roll over and go to stand up. "Fine, but at least help me with my leggings. They are too tight. I need them off." She looks over at me with pleading eyes.

Standing up, I dip my fingers into her leggings and slowly pull them down. Past her hips, then her thighs, her sex is right in front of my face. It's begging me to touch it, and making it even more difficult, I can smell her arousal.

"Mmm that's much better," she says as soon as I get her leggings off.

I try my hardest not to look at her, but I'm a weak man. My eyes roam over her body. Her bra and panties are a basic white cotton. Taking in those perky breasts, flat stomach, and thick thighs, I take a deep breath. I'd love to bury my face in all of them.

Catching my eyes, Alice slowly reaches behind her to unclasp her bra. "No, don't," I say, but I'm too late. My eyes land on her perfect tits. God help me. I'm not strong enough to resist her. I don't move. I just look at her.

She walks over towards me slowly. All signs of drunk Alice, gone. All I can do is watch as she stalks towards me. With every step, her boobs move ever so slightly. They draw me in like a trance, and I can't look away.

It seems like hours until she reaches me, and once she does her eyes are searing into mine. "I don't mind if you look. I wouldn't mind it if you touched either." She grabs my left hand and slides it up to cup her right boob.

"Fuck, Alice." This girl is really testing my willpower. It's starting to run out. Unable to help myself, I start to knead her boob. They feel like marshmallows under my hands.

My mouth salivates at the need to have them in my mouth. Her head rolls back as she lets out a slight moan.

Good lord, this woman.

Feeling slight pain from my dick pressing against my jeans, I go to adjust myself.

"Let me help you with that," she whispers as she goes to rub me outside of my jeans.

"Alice, you're drunk." I grab her hand before she can touch me.

"I'm not anymore. I'm pretty tipsy, but I'm not drunk, Logan." She presses herself into me. The movement makes her boob smash into my hands even more. Her pelvis is up against mine, and I can feel her breathing pick up.

I should walk away. I should drop my hand, turn my back from her, and walk out that door. I don't want to be that mistake she made when she was drunk. I want to be that happy memory she thinks back on.

"Please, Logan." Her please is my undoing. I can't say no to her. Letting go of her hand, I allow her to touch me. She runs her hand down my stiffening dick.

"Fuck, Alice."

I lean my head back and moan at the feel of her hand on me. I can just picture her stroking me on her knees. My dick needs to be released from its confines, but I don't move. This is all up to her.

With wavering hands, she starts to unbutton my jeans. Part of me is praising the heavens above, but the other part of me is wondering if this is right?

"Touch me, Logan. Please," she begs once again, and I lose all control. Grabbing my zipper, I rip it open and pull out my throbbing dick. Relief rushes through me. That zipper was really starting to dig in.

Grabbing both of her tits into my hands I familiarize myself with them. Then, with desperation, I slide one into my mouth. Rolling her nipple between my teeth, I hear her moan.

Lost in the moment, I grab her thighs and wrap her legs around me as I lay her onto the bed. Crawling on top of her, I settle between her legs.

Then, I claim her lips once again. Only this time, I shove my tongue down her throat. I want to taste her. I want her to taste me and remember it in the morning.

I grind myself between her legs and I'm treated to the sweetest moan. I want to be inside of her, dragging out every last moan she has to offer.

Breaking our kiss for a moment to look at her beautiful face, I look down at her. Her breathing is as fast as mine is. I can feel her heart slamming against her chest just as mine is.

I want this, but I want her to remember this in the morning. "I'm sorry, Alice. I just can't keep going. I want to be fucking you every way possible right now, but I don't want our first time to be a drunken fling."

Her breathing slows and her eyes start to get heavy. "Come on, let's get into bed. She doesn't fight me this time. Either the adrenaline is gone or the alcohol is wearing off. Either way, she starts to relax into my arms.

I hold her back against my chest. Hearing her breathing start to set a steady pace, I know she is asleep. "Sleep well, Alice." I kiss her forehead, tuck her in, and go out to sleep on her couch.

Chapter 9 Alice

Rolling over, I see the sun peeking into my bedroom.

What time is it?

My eyes struggle to open, my mouth feels like sand, and I'm naked. Memories of last night flood my mind. Leaving the bar with Logan, him not letting that guy touch me at all, undressing in front of him, and me throwing myself at him.

I cover my face with my hands from embarrassment.

I can't believe you did that!

Memories of Logan's lips on mine heat my belly. His touch on my boobs still linger making my nipples pucker.

Shaking off the memory, I get out of bed and walk towards the kitchen.

I need some water.

Not bothering to get dressed, I use the restroom then walk out into the living room.

"Damn it, Alice. Don't you ever wear clothes? You're killing me." I hear someone say. I scream as I turn around and see Logan laying on my couch. His chest is bare. He looks to be naked under a thin blanket I had on the couch.

Covering my boobs instinctively, I march over to him. "What the hell are you doing here?"

He stands up slowly, letting the blanket fall over himself. My eyes drift to the blanket, following its movements until it hits the floor. Thankfully, he is wearing a tight pair of briefs.

Once again, memories of last night engulf my thoughts. I remember rubbing his dick through his jeans. I remember pleading with him to let me, and I remember that kiss. Holy hell do I remember that kiss.

"Alice?" I hear Logan interrupt my thoughts. "You okay?" He asks with a grin. His morning wood is on clear display, but he doesn't seem to care.

What is happening?

I should run back to my room and put some clothes on. Why haven't I moved yet? Why can't I remember how to walk? "What?" I finally remember how to speak at least.

"I said, I stayed over to make sure you were okay. Are you okay?" He starts talking towards me. One, two, three, four steps closer. His hand brushes away my rat's nest of a hairdo from my face.

"Yeah, I'm good. I should probably go get dressed though. And you should probably cover that up." I point down at his member. It's pressed against my stomach, and I'm having a really difficult time focusing.

"Does this bother you? It didn't seem to last night." He tilts my chin up to meet his eyes. "If I recall correctly, you were begging me to let you touch it. It's clearly ready, but now you're shying away?" I look back down at him. He's twisting his hips back and forth, causing his dick to run along my stomach.

"You can reach in there and grab it if you want. Maybe we can be friends with benefits," he says with the most serious look.

Is he for real? He wants to be friends with benefits? I haven't heard that term since I was in my early years of college.

Friends with benefits?

Could I do that? If I was going to have casual sex with anyone, I would probably want it to be with Logan. I trust him. He is my safe space. Even though we have only known each other for two months, he really is like my best friend already. I guess that will happen when you're spending all your waking hours with someone.

Sorry Becks. I still love you.

Becks has been so busy at RedLights Co. I haven't seen her since my last day of work. I can't believe it's been that long. Those jerks are making her do two jobs. Thankfully, they did give her a raise.

I need to call her.

"Alice," Logan says again. "Are you still drunk?"

"No, I was just thinking about what you said."

"I was just messing with you, Alice," he says as he goes to grab his shirt.

"You were just messing with me about being friends with benefits? Were you messing with me last night when you laid me on the bed and settled between my legs? Or when you couldn't take your hands off my tits? Or your lips…"

"I get it. I was weak. I mean, look at you. You were pleading with me, but I stopped eventually," he interrupts me before I can finish.

I'm still cupping my boobs to hide them from Logan. I want to drop them to my side and see what he does, but I'm nervous about what he will say now that we are both sober. He says he was just joking about being friends with benefits, but maybe he is on to something.

I mean, we both need to get laid, but we don't want to be with each other in a relationship. We trust each other completely. I don't think Logan would make it awkward. I'd be more likely to be the awkward one, but I think Logan would help with that too.

Taking a deep breath, I drop my hands and watch as Logan's eyes go wide. His mouth drops open, and I can't help but smile. "What were you saying about being weak?"

"Alice, I'm warning you. You need to go back into your room and put your damn clothes on," he says without taking his eyes off my boobs. Instinctively, he grabs himself and gives it a pull for relief.

I step closer to him. "Or you'll do what?" I whisper against his mouth as I stand on my tippy toes. I'm baiting him. We always tease each other, but this is different. And we both know it.

We are at a stand still. His eyes are on me, and my eyes are on him. It's a game of chicken. Who will move first?

"What are you doing, Alice?"

"I'm taking you up on your *friends with benefits* offer."

"I never offered that. I was messing with you."

"So you're saying I should just put my clothes back on? You wouldn't be the least bit interested in having an arrangement together?" I watch as his eyes roam over my body once again. I'm pretty sure he would lose it if I were to touch him. Just like he did last night.

I kind of wish he hadn't been such a good guy last night. Then, we would have already had sex, and we could continue with this instead of me having to talk him into it.

"I'm saying if you don't put your clothes on something is probably going to happen because I'm about to lose my restraint." To my surprise, he reaches over and grabs his t-shirt and pulls it over my head.

"There, I can finally think now. I can't think with this head when you're naked," he says, pointing to the side of his temple. Maybe he's right. I guess we should probably talk about it first.

Once his shirt is covering the rest of my body, I walk to the kitchen and get my much needed water. Without asking, I bring him a glass too. I don't think he drank as much as I did, but I'm sure he could use it.

"Thanks." He takes the glass of water. I study him as he gulps the whole glass down in ten seconds.

"Thirsty?" I question as I drink my water. I drink it quickly, but not as fast as Logan just did. I don't think I could drink that fast if I was in the desert for three days.

"I am," he says as he looks at my bare legs. I'm guessing he isn't talking about the water.

Reading his thoughts I ask, "Do I need to put some pants on too?"

He tilts his head still looking at my legs. "Here, just put this on." He gives me the banket as we both sit down. I snuggle into the couch as Logan sits right next to me. The heat from his body warms me. It's nice.

Looking over at him, he has his head back on the couch as if he is thinking about something. My eyes drift down to his bare chest. Letting them linger there for a while since he can't see me, I imagine running my hands over his sexy body. I admire his toned pecs and shoulders. His muscles aren't washboard abs, but he is still very fit. You can tell he works out and takes care of himself. I can't say I don't like that he has something to grab on to.

Continuing my trail down his body, I notice he is still hard. It's not as noticeable as it is when he is standing up, but you can clearly see it. "I think you need some too." I hand him some of the blanket. He takes it willingly and covers himself. I'm a little sad to see the view go.

"Thanks." After a few minutes of silence, Logan starts talking again. "Now that we are both mostly clothed and can properly think..." He doesn't finish his sentence. He only looks at me as if he wants me to continue, so I do.

"I think we could sleep together and still just be friends."

"That simple, huh?" I mean, yeah. Why can't it be that simple?

"Why not? You need sex. I need sex. Neither one of us wants that kind of relationship with each other, so why not? I trust you, and I'm pretty sure you trust me."

"I think I do," he says jokingly.

"Then why not?"

"You know this kind of thing never goes well. The friends always end up either not being friends anymore, or they realize they have loved each other all along. I wouldn't want you falling head over heels for me, Alice." The cocky Logan is back I see.

Turning to face him, I put my legs in his lap. "Don't you already know....I'm madly in love with you. I can't live without you, Logan." He pushes my legs off of him, gets up and starts walking towards the bathroom, but I don't stop talking.

"Please don't leave me. I need you." I keep going until he has shut the bathroom door. I hear him in the bathroom laughing which makes me laugh. "See, nothing is going to change. I've felt your dick, made out with you, and I still find you annoying. I think we're good."

"Fine." Did he just agree? I jump up and run towards the half bath he is in.

"So that's a yes?"

"We still need to set some rules, but yes. Now leave me alone so I can take a shit." Ugh, my bathroom is going to stink, but I can't help but smile.

"I'm going to get some. I'm going to get some," I sing as I march to my room.

I should probably take a shower. I'm sure Logan's going to be in there forever. Turning on the water as hot as my skin can bare it, I let it fall over me. It's extremely relaxing.

My mind drifts to last night. *Please, Logan.* The moment he let go and kissed me. The feel of him between my legs. The way he grinded on me. My own hand starts its descent. Finding its destination between my legs, I let out a moan as I start to circle my clit. I imagine Logan touching me. I wonder how good he is at it? I'm sure he is pretty experienced.

"Can't even wait?" I hear Logan say as he peers in at me. I can't help but scream and throw my washcloth at him. Turning around as fast as possible, I cover myself.

"What are you doing in here?" I squeal.

"I needed a shower, and you only have one." I watch from over my shoulder. He swiftly pulls off his briefs and his dick springs to life.

Holy shit.

I take in a deep breath and turn back around. His dick looks so good, I want to eat it up right now. I want to drop to the floor and suck on it like a sucker until I find the gooey center.

I feel his body invade my space. The shower is a regular sized tub, so there isn't a lot of space. His hands go to my side. I can feel them soothing my skin, but I don't dare move. My chest is pounding. My breathing is noticeably picking up. I'm sure I'm already getting wet.

"You said something about rules? I'm guessing showering together isn't on them?" I hear him hum into my ear. The noise vibrates his chest, and it sends a tingle down to my swollen nub.

"It is on there."

"Then why are you in here?" I push myself against him, encouraging him to continue. I want so much more.

"It says we have to shower together." I start laughing.

"So anytime I need to shower, I have to call you and wait the ten minutes it takes for you to reach my apartment?" That's ridiculous, but I know he's joking.

"That sounds like a good idea. Don't you think?" I roll my eyes even though he can't see me.

"I thought you said we needed to be dressed to talk about this? What happened to not being able to think if I'm naked?" I rub my ass against him which earns me a hiss. And damn it if it isn't the hottest sound I've ever heard.

"I definitely can't focus if you're doing that, so stop it." He swats me on the ass, and a moan slips from my lips. Heat pours into me as he rubs the spot he just smacked. I cannot believe he just did that. Not that I'm complaining. It felt surprisingly good.

"I guess you liked that." I nod my head. I can feel my head starting to spin from the high I'm experiencing. "Like I said before, if you don't stop the teasing I'm going to make you pay." I have to admit, I like the sound of that.

"Just like you can't focus when I'm naked, I can't not tease you if you are." I still can't believe Logan is in the shower with me, naked. I'm sure as soon as we have sex,

I'll be telling him to get off of me. But right now, all I can think about is having his hands on me.

"You're right. We should get washed up, and then we can talk after we're dressed." He goes to grab the washcloth I threw at him, but I take it from him. Pushing him back against the wall, I squirt soap onto the rag and start to rub him with it. His eyes roam my body because this is the first time he is seeing me completely naked. They land between my legs, and I can feel my wetness start to slide down me.

"Fuck, Alice." He bellows as I drop the rag and start to soap up his body without it. My hands slide over his chest, lingering on his nipples. I want those in my mouth too. His chest rises and falls much faster than it was before. I'd say he likes this.

Taking my time on each of his muscles in his arms, I make my way down to his abs. I may be teasing him, but I'm also teasing myself. I want nothing more than to grab his dick that is standing at attention for me, but I stop myself.

Looking up at him as I drop to my knees, his eyes are no longer a pale green. They are red with lust. "Alice, what are you doing?" He grabs a fist full of my hair, forcing me to look up at him.

"I'm washing your legs. Why? What did you think I was doing?" I very slowly lick my lips. My tongue gets so close to the tip of his dick, he sucks in all of the air that's left in the shower. He wants this so bad. Good, because so do I.

He grabs the base of his erection with his free hand. I can see the mental dilemma in his eyes. *Do I shove my dick in her mouth or do I wait until we have had our conversation.*

Making his decision even harder on him, I part my lips. Fully ready to accept him should he choose to go that way, I wait. "Damn it, Alice. Fuck." He really is struggling with his decision, but it's no fun making it easy on him.

After a few more seconds, he releases my hair and himself. "I'm clean enough for now, it's your turn." He pulls me up off of my knees. I'm shocked he didn't give in. I mean, my mouth was basically touching his dick, and he still pulled away. He must have more willpower than I thought.

He pulls me to change sides with him. Meeting his fiery red eyes, I see a different Logan than I'm used to. This one is hot. This one is full of need. He has let down all his cocky walls, and I just see him.

Grabbing the soap bottle, he starts to lather his hands together. Oh boy, it really is my turn. I am really good with teasing, but I don't have the willpower Logan so clearly does.

He starts on my shoulders. Quickly making his way down my arms and over to my sides. His hands are rougher than they were last night. I guess it's all that built up tension. He really needs to release that. I'm tempted to grab his dick, rules be damned, but I don't. I relish in this torture. Only, it's not very tortuous yet.

Clearly speaking too soon, he grabs both my boobs in his large hands. My boobs are on the smaller side, probably only a B cup, so his hands cover them nicely. "Are you thinking about these in my mouth?" His voice startles me.

I can't speak so I simply nod. Of course I am. I'm thinking about several things that could go in his mouth.

He pinches both of my nipples at the same time. The pleasure it sends down my body is head spinning. I want more, but he releases me. "Those are going to be so much fun to play with."

I can't take it anymore. I need him. Reaching out, I try to grab his dick that is begging me to touch it, but he catches my hand before I can. "It's still my turn, Alice."

"Should I beg? That seemed to work last night." I go to reach for him again, but he stops me.

"Just stand there and be good," he says pointing a finger at me.

Rolling my eyes, I decide I'll be good for now. Grabbing more soap, he rubs one leg then another. Moving up past my knee and up my thigh, his fingers continue to roam.

Pulling on my thighs, I spread my legs out just a little. I watch him as he runs his fingers up the inner part of my legs. He is so close to the apex of my thighs, but he isn't quick where I crave him. His fingers touch every part of me other than my most needy part.

I'm pretty sure I'm visibly throbbing by now. "Logan." My voice comes out raspy. It's full of need, full of desire. I want to beg him to take me right here in the small shower, but he doesn't.

"What's the matter, Alice? Is your core clenching, begging to feel my fingers slide inside? Is your clit throbbing, aching to have my tongue on it?" His words are dirty, but they are completely true.

"Please." I watch his hooded eyes. They are just as needy as mine are. I will say it's a nice view seeing him on his knee for me, but I want him to stand up and take me. I want to feel his arms around me as he shoves himself inside of me.

Without saying anything, he grabs the washcloth and continues washing the rest of himself. When he gets to his dick, I whimper. He strokes it once, twice, three times before letting go. "Don't even think about it." I give him an evil stare.

Reaching for my loofah that's hanging on the on and off spout, I start to wash myself. His eyes watching every move my hand makes, all while still washing himself. He finishes before I do, but continues to watch me.

Turning around, I bend over to wash my feet. My ass is shoved right into his crotch. "Alright, I think you're done." Logan grabs the loofah from me and rinses the rest of the soap off. Hanging it on the spout, he brings me under the water to rinse off. Looking me over, he turns the water off.

"Get some clothes on, and get to your bedroom." Horny Logan is so bossy. I love it!

Logan walks right out to my bedroom. Then, he is out of view. "You good with me tossing my clothes in the wash for a speed wash?" I hear him yell out.

"Of course," I reply.

Once I dry off, I pull my hair up into a towel. Grabbing my silk robe, I slip it on as I make my way to my room.

Logan is laying on my bed, arms behind his head, ankles crossed, and eyes on me. His towel lays lazily over himself.

"So I had to put clothes on, but you didn't? I eye him up and down.

"First off, what you put on is not clothes. Secondly, I don't have any clean clothes here, so I'll be naked here until they are washed. I hear my washer going. I guess he found what he needed.

"So what are these rules you speak of, Spencer? Because you're starting to lose your charm." I am so sexually frustrated right now, I'm worried I'm going to go off on him. Sitting down by his feet, I cross my legs applesauce style.

His eyes go right down to my bare sex before I can cover it. Taking in a deep breath, his eyes come back up to mine. "Let's talk about it. What's something that is important to you?"

"Before any of this can go further, are you clean?" I know Logan is far from innocent, but I don't think I have to worry about it.

"Oh for sure. I always keep this guy wrapped up." He rubs his dick over the towel, and of course I can't help but watch him.

"Good," I say after licking my lips. I feel like a hungry animal, playing with my prey before I eat it.

"What about you?" He nods towards me.

"Little o'me?" I ask, pretending to be offended. "I got tested two months ago at my yearly visit. I'm good. Plus, I'm on the pill."

"Good. Are you saying I don't need to wrap it up?" He asks hopefully.

"That's not what I said." He gives me a pouty look. I guess if we are both clean, and I am on the pill it probably would be fine. I've heard stories of girls getting pregnant while on the pill. I really do not want that to happen.

"Alright, I'll wear one. So what now?" I think for a while. There has to be more to it. We need guidelines.

Several minutes go by before I speak. "We each get 3 no questions asked fucks. No matter where we are, who we are with, if the other calls, we have to go."

"So like a booty call?" He asks.

"If you want to call it that, but I don't think that. It's an agreement between two friends."

"Can we fuck other people while we are doing this?" Logan asks. That's a good question. I don't really like the idea of having sex with someone while they are having sex with someone else, but I also don't want to tell him he can't have sex with someone else.

"How about, if we are wanting to have sex with someone else, we let the other person know. Not asking for permission, just informing. If the person decides they no longer want to do this then we void the deal."

"So you're saying if I call you and tell you I'm about to screw some chick you can decide to cancel our agreement?"

"Yes." He looks at me for a moment.

"Deal. Take off your robe." He goes to reach for me, but I back away.

"Are you wanting to use one of your times?"

"We can't get a freebie to start us out?" I shake my head.

"I think you'd be trying to get all of them as freebies. That's the whole point of the agreement. We only get to have sex six times in total. That will help with long term effects." My thoughts are, if we only have sex six times we probably won't develop feelings for each other. Plus, six times probably won't last us for very long. It still gives us a chance to meet someone we are actually interested in.

"Damn, you say it like I'm a disease. What about a tester?"

"What the hell is that?" He grabs my legs and pulls me onto his lap. My robe rides up my body. He can't see me, but my bare sex is right on him. The only thing separating us is his towel.

"Testing the waters so to speak. We won't have sex, but we can see how in sync we are to make sure this is going to work." His hands roam up the insides of my legs. His fingers an inch away from where I want him. He's waiting for me to agree.

"I have a feeling once we start, we won't be able to stop," I say as I roll my hips on him. He sucks in air at my movements, and I can feel him hardening fast underneath me.

"Haven't I proven several times already that I have self control?" That is true, but he isn't the one I'm worried about.

Leaning down, my robe displays my bare chest to him. Before I lose my nerve, I allow my lips to graze his. That's all the consent he needs.

Chapter 10 Logan

My left hand comes up to her head, forcing her down harder onto me. I need to feel her, even if it's just her mouth on me. She molds against my body, kissing me harder. My right hand goes to her tits, and she lets out a delicious moan.

My tongue dives into her mouth, not waiting for permission this time. I'm taking what I want this time.

But you have to stop eventually.

The reminder goes off in my head. I may have to stop before we have sex, but I don't have to stop myself now. Rolling her nipple between my finger and thumb, I pinch it. Another moan releases from Alice's mouth, and it's music to my ears.

She grabs at my towel, trying to move it from between us. If that towel is moved, I will be fucking her. I won't be able to stop. No amount of willpower will stop my dick from sliding into her wetness if she is grinding her pussy against my bare dick. It's simply impossible. "That needs to stay there for now."

She gives up for now, but I know her. She will try again. Her lips move from mine over to my jaw, down my neck, and to my chest.

Fuck

I know where this is going, and I can't stop her. She continues her descent down past my belly button. Crawling between my legs, I release her. She looks up at me with an evil grin. She knows exactly what I'm thinking.

"I have to remove the towel at some point. You did say you wanted to test the waters, right?" My words coming back to bite me in the ass. I give her a subtle nod, and she rips the towel off in one motion. Her eyes go wide with excitement the moment my dick stops bouncing.

Yeah, you're going to have fun with that, aren't you?

Leaning back, she watches me as she, I'm assuming, admires me. Reaching up, I pull the tie on her robe. I watch as it falls open, and she shrugs it off. I've seen her naked in the shower, but this is different. She is higher up and open for me. I can see the glistening from between her lips, showing just how wet she is for me.

For me.

Six times. I get six times with her after this. I guess if this is how I can have her, it's better than nothing. I will take all of her that I can get. I'm not sure when my feelings started for her, but it was probably right after that first kiss.

Reaching down, I run my finger through her folds. I can't stop myself.

Yup, so fucking wet, and so fucking ready. For me.

Her head leans back and lets out a moan of pure, sweet ecstasy. Greedily she grinds her hips forward. My fingers move in circles as I watch her play with her nipples.

"Damnit, Alice." Watching her touch her own tits is going to send me over the edge, and she isn't even touching me yet.

When I caught her in the shower touching herself, I wanted to replace her hand with mine. I wanted to give her the pleasure she so desperately desires.

Sinking a finger inside of her, we moan at the same time. If my finger feels this good, it's going to feel phenomenal when I slip my dick inside of her. Pumping inside of her, I add another finger. "Oh my gosh, Logan."

Using my thumb to rub her clit as I slam my fingers inside of her, she lets out another moan. I could listen to this all day. I could watch this all day. I could do this all day.

"Logan," she mumbles. I can tell she's close. Fuck, I can't wait to hear what she sounds like when she cums. I'm going to record it in my head and play it back for months to come.

"Cum for me, Alice. I want to hear you. I want you to scream my name." And that is exactly what she does. Her head arches back, giving me a great view of her tits. Grabbing one of them, I pinch her nipple as she rides her orgasm wave. The earthquake that just ripped through her sends aftershocks as I pull my fingers out of her.

So good. So beautiful.

Pulling my hand all the way out of her, I get the urge to taste her. That's next on the list. I'd love to hear how intense the second orgasm is coming from those lips. Before I get a chance, she is moving down my body. Grabbing the base of my dick, she gives it a few soft pumps.

A hiss comes from my lips. Even her hand feels unbelievable. Everything about this girl is feeling too good. I'm going to be ruined after six times.

Fuck six times. I want more.

Keeping her eyes on me, she leans down and licks the pebble of pre-cum off my head. My whole body jerks at the heat of her mouth. Following the motion of her hand, her mouth covers my head. With a loud suck, she pops it out of her mouth. She's teasing me again.

Grabbing her hair, I shove her mouth down onto me. When she gags, I back off a little. I didn't mean to be that rough. She is driving me crazy.

Watching her bob her head up and down, she rolls my base with her hand. I usually pride myself in lasting a while, but this girl is going to make me cum like a sixteen year old Logan.

Pausing for a moment, she looks up at me. My dick still in her mouth. Damn, it's a beautiful sight. "Wait, I thought we weren't supposed to have sex?" Alice comes off my dick just enough to mumble those words.

"It doesn't count," I quickly say as I guide her back on me. If she stopped right now, I think I might cry. Thankfully, she keeps going. Sucking and pulling even harder than she did before.

I will not put my dick in her pussy today. I will not put my dick in her pussy today.

I keep telling myself because I told her I would stop before it came to that, but right now I'm not sure I can keep that promise. It's taking everything I have not to push her back onto the bed and bury myself deep inside her right now.

Picturing me being deep inside her, I cum hard. I hear her gag as my cum shoots to the back of her throat, but she doesn't stop until she pumps every drop out of me. Reaching beside us, I hand her the towel.

"Thanks," she wipes her face off. Did she just swallow me?

"My turn," I say with a devilish grin. She lets out a squeal as I roll her onto her back. Pushing her knees up, I open them wide for me. Instinctively she goes to hide herself. It's really bright in her room, and I can see all of her. And I love it.

"You better move that hand," I say as I settle between her legs. "I plan on memorizing you so I can jerk off to it once our six times are up."

"Oh my gosh, stop." She laughs, but she knows it's true.

Not wasting another moment, I lick her clit softly. Her hands go straight to my hair and she pulls me closer. That's exactly how I know when I'm at the right spot. The hands always go to the hair, and they always pull harder. My girl is no different when it comes to that. In every other way, she is different. She is special. Only, she isn't my girl.

Shaking out those thoughts, I focus on her sweet tasting lips. Reaching under her ass, I pull her towards me.

She is propped up and open for me, but she doesn't seem to mind this time. She's my meal for the day, and I want to savor every bite.

Shoving my tongue inside of her, I wrap my hand around her leg and roll her clit around. "Ah, Logan. Right there. Please don't stop," she pants. I'll never stop. Not until she tells me to.

Harder and harder I drive my tongue into her. Feeling her hips bucking, I can tell she wants it harder. Sliding my tongue up to her clit, I shove two fingers inside of her. I know she's wet and ready for me. "Oh, yes. Yes." Her back arches higher and higher until she drops it as her orgasm shatters through her body.

Feeling her clench around my fingers again is heavenly. My dick is pulsing at the thought. He thinks it's his turn.

Sorry buddy. Not today.

I climb to her side and pull her head onto my chest. Once my breathing slows down, I tilt her head back to look at me. "So, do you think it's good enough to continue?" I ask, back to my sarcastic self, even with a boner. Usually it takes me a good hour to be ready again, but not this time. Not with Alice. I was ready from the moment I tasted her sweet arousal.

She laughs and nods her head. "Yes, we can definitely do that again."

Kissing her forehead, I go to get up to put my clothes in the dryer. "Good," I say with a smile.

Once I change out my clothes, I climb back into bed with her. Having her in my arms feel right. It's what we were made for.

We sit like this for 30 minutes. We don't talk. We just enjoy each other. That is until she starts drawing circles along my skin. They start on my chest. Circling my nipples, she continues down to my hips.

Taking a deep breath, I go to stand up because if I don't put some distance between us, I'm going to use one of my times already. I need to pace myself.

"I should probably go. I have a ton of shit I need to do this weekend," I admit while walking out to the laundry area. My clothes are done by now, thankfully.

When I return to her room fully clothed, she only put on her robe. Knowing she is naked under that robe does not help my situation. I tried to hide it the best I could, but you can still clearly see I'm supporting a boner.

"Jeez, use me and leave," Alice jokes.

"Can't have you getting too attached, ya know. Bitches be crazy for this," I point towards my body. Alice busts out laughing. I'm glad we are still us.

"Get out of here before I fall in love." I watch her as she falls back onto the bed, ignoring me as I leave.

Chapter 11 Alice

I'm pretty sure Logan is trying to play it cool. I grabbed my phone several times today to ask him to come over for a quick screw. Instead, I sent him a few sexy photos of my new bra and panty set I picked up while at the mall. He didn't even ask for more. What's up with that?

He did say he has more self control than I do, and I think he is right. I'm probably going to have to ask him for sex first to get this going. That's fine. I'm not above it, but I'll at least try to hold out until tomorrow. I can always tease him though.

Me: What are you doing?

I send a text to Logan hoping he's free. Although, our rules are the other has to come no matter what they are doing. I wonder if I text him while he was at the gym, right after working out. That would be hot.

It takes him about twenty minutes to reply. I'm washing the dishes when he does.

Logan: Is this a booty call?

Oh good lord. Is he ever serious? No. No, he is not. How did his mother deal with him growing up?

Me: Nope. I just wanted to know the well being of my good friend. Is he there?

Who am I kidding? I'm just as sarcastic as he is. That's probably why we get along so well.

Logan: Nope. Just me.

Me: Well when you find that hot guy that was here earlier, let me know.

It's almost 10:00 p.m, so I'm already in bed.

Logan: He is pretty hot, right?

Cocky Logan is here.

Me: I just wanted to let him know I was about to go to bed. In that bed he tasted me in a few hours ago. I'm still not satisfied. I may need to use my vibrator.

He replies immediately.

Logan: Lies. Prove it.

Me: Turning my phone on silent. Tell him I said good night.

I let my phone on *silent mode* so he can see the warning at the bottom of the text thread.

Logan: Don't play with me, woman.

Ten minutes later he texts me again.

Logan: Ah come on. You did me dirty. What am I going to do with this?

He sends me a picture of his hard length under his briefs. I want to respond so badly. I want to tell him to get his ass over here, but I can't.

Logan: Fine. I guess I'll be taking care of this myself tonight. Sleep well temptress.

I look at his picture for a few more minutes, and now I'm horny again thanks to him. Reaching for my vibrator, I use it for a few minutes. Frustration hits me because it's not hitting that spot Logan was reaching with his long, magnificent fingers.

Needing to work off this frustration, I put on my running clothes and head down to our gym. I almost never workout this late. I almost never workout in our gym. Our apartment complex is huge. It probably has over 10,000 units, and they only provide one gym. It's usually packed. I'm crossing my fingers it's not tonight.

I jog over to the gym which is about two hundred yards away. Once I open the door I sigh in relief. There is only one other girl in the gym, and it looks like she is finishing up.

We exchange a smile as she wipes off her damp forehead. That's the best part of working out. I love the sweating. After you sweat everything out, you feel like a new person. I should probably do this more often. If I came late, I wouldn't have to deal with as many people.

Jumping onto the treadmill, I don't bother with the headphones. Since no one else is in here, I use my phone speakers to turn on my workout playlist. I listen to it on loud as I jog. Clearing my mind, I fall into pace with the beat.

Before I realize it, I've already ran over a mile. I usually can't run much more than two miles.

Feeling that familiar burn once I hit just before the two mile mark, I start to slow down for my cool off walk. Even after my run, thoughts of Logan still won't leave my mind.

Pulling off my t-shirt, I wipe my face, arms, and stomach down as I grab my phone and water and head out of the gym.

" Fancy meeting you here," I hear a somewhat familiar voice say. It causes me to jump when I hear him sneak up on me. My phone was on loud so I didn't hear anyone come in. When I turn around, I'm face-to-face with Ryder.

Shock overtakes my face, silencing me. "I assume you live here? Or you're really bad at stalking me. It took you entirely too long to find me." Ryder is here. He is standing inside the gym of my apartment complex. Is this really happening?

What are the odds that he lives here, comes to the gym at this time, and runs into me? They have to be like 1 to 100,000. "Oh my gosh," is the only thing I can say. I'm probably the most shocked I have ever been in my life. I mean, Ryder is here.

Thinking back to that night, I get a little nervous being alone with him in this room. Not nervous for the fact that he would mean harm to me, but nervous for the fact that his hands have been inside me.

Whose fingers did I enjoy more? Logan or Ryder? I honestly cannot choose. They both felt unreal. They both got me off skillfully. They both made me feel things, but Logan is just my friend. A friend I just started a deal with. A deal I'd like to finish. I'm honestly looking forward to knowing what Logan will feel like inside of me, but now I can't help but wonder how Ryder would feel. If his fingers felt that good, I imagine he knows how to use his dick too.

"Are you okay?" He asks with concerned eyes. That's sweet.

"Yes, I'm so sorry. I am just in complete shock to see you. I never thought I'd see you again," I admit.

"Did you not want to see me again? I can leave if you'd like?" I don't think he's joking. He would really leave if I didn't want to see him? I guess that's good to know. It's good to know he would honor my wishes, but I don't want him to leave. At least, I don't think I do.

I wonder what Logan would think about this? Would he mind? Would he get jealous? No, I don't think so. We're just friends. That's why we made the deal. If we meet someone and want to screw, we just end the deal. I can't end our deal already. We haven't even started it. I can't say I wouldn't be tempted to screw Ryder though.

"No, Ryder. I don't want you to leave. I'm sorry if I made you feel that way. Apparently, this is your gym too," I say quickly.

"Yeah, going on two years. How about you? How long have you lived here?"

"I moved in right after I graduated college about four years ago. I really love it here," I say with a smile. I still can't believe I'm talking to Ryder and he lives in my complex.

"So you're what? 25?" He asks.

"Yes, I just turned 25 in December. How old are you?" I would bet he is my age.

"28." That night at the bar, I wouldn't have guessed he was that much older than me, but up close, in the light, he seems older.

"I would have guessed younger." I feel like most people want to hear that. No one wants to hear they think they look older.

"So, which building do you live in?" He asks. I hesitate telling him. That's just what I need, him showing up when Logan is there. Neither one of them would understand the other.

"I'm actually in building 7." It's weird having a conversation with a guy with little to zero joking. It's been a while since I've done that. With Logan, everything is a joke. Don't get me wrong, I love that about him. That's why we are great friends, but this feels different with Ryder.

"Nice. I'm in 13. I have a co-worker that's your neighbor in 6." I notice his eyes trail down to my bra. I should be embarrassed, but it's a sports bra so it covers just as much as some of my crop tops. "I like your sports bra," Ryder says as he touches the material on my collarbone. That action surprises me, but it doesn't bother me.

"Thanks. It's soft isn't it?" He nods as he runs his finger down the side of it. It sends a shiver down my spine as I remember where that finger has been.

"So have you been feeling better since I saw you last?" I'm not sure exactly what he means? I don't think I was feeling bad when I saw him last.

"What do you mean?" I look at him confused.

"The last time I saw you, you were struggling with need." Oh my gosh. My cheeks go bright red. I can feel the heat. Thankfully, my skin was already red from the run. Hopefully he doesn't notice.

My hand goes to my face. "Oh you know. I've been doing okay." I really don't want to tell him that earlier today I had my best friend's fingers deep inside me, so I'm doing pretty great actually.

"Does that mean you haven't been needing any release?" I can't tell if he is flirting with me. Just like at the bar. He was so serious and matter of fact. "That either means you're getting someone else to do it, or you found a really good toy."

I am completely mortified. What am I supposed to say to that? He must see my hesitation. "You don't have to be shy with me, Alice." Wait, how did he know my name? I never told him.

"How did you know my name?" He shakes his head.

"Your friend told my sister. Apparently she talked about you a lot. Now, don't change the subject. I genuinely want to know. Have you found someone to get you off, or did you find a new toy?" I think about it for a minute. Does he really want to know the truth?

"I guess I would say a little of both." He gives me a questioning look, so I tell him the story. I tell him about my best friend and how we first met. I tell him about our deal we made that we haven't really started yet. I even tell him that just earlier today we had a test run.

Ryder stands there the whole time, intrigued. "This sounds fun. So if you called him right now, he'd have to come fuck you in the gym?" I guess that is the deal.

"Yes."

"I must say, I'm a little jealous. I was hoping you'd say you needed some more help. We could have a lot of fun trying to satisfy you. I have a feeling we'd have to try a lot." I can feel my breathing picking up. He wants to touch me again?

"Let me see your phone." He interrupts my thoughts. I assume he is wanting to give me his number so I open my contacts and hand it to him. He quickly types in his number and hands me back my phone.

He steps closer to me and kisses me on the cheek. "I hope our paths cross again soon, Alice. If you get bored with your little game you're playing, and you decide you want more, give me a call.

Ryder walks over to the treadmill, pops his headphones in, turns to smile at me, then starts his run.

Did I hear him right? *If you get bored with your little game you're playing, and you decide you want more, give me a call.* Does that mean he is looking for more than just a hookup? Do I want more than just hooking up? I guess that's something I need to figure out first.

I spend most of the next morning thinking of Ryder and our conversation. Was he just blowing smoke up my ass, or would he actually be interested in trying something more with me?

He doesn't even know me. He's a stranger. One I had a very mind blowing orgasm with. One I'd like to revisit, but what about Logan?

On one hand, I really enjoyed Logan's fingers and tongue on me. Good lord that tongue of his did some amazing work. On the other hand, I'd love to know how

Ryder's tongue would feel on me. I feel so wrong thinking about the two of them like this…at the same time. But it's not like I'm actually dating either one of them.

Ryder knows I have a deal going with Logan. He still seemed interested though. I wonder if he'd still be interested after I have sex with Logan? I don't want to regret not having fun with Logan, but damn it, Ryder is sexy. I know he would be a good time. Plus, he might give me more than just great sex.

Am I still going through with this with Logan? Not only did I already agree to it, but I genuinely want to know how Logan feels inside of me. Does that make me slutty? If it does, oh well. I've been thinking about it for days. I mean, why do I have to choose right now?

Grabbing my phone off the bed, I send a text.

Me: Want to do something later? I'm bored.

Do I want sex? Yes! Have I ever been good at asking for it? No!

Logan: Are you wanting me to do you later?

"Ugh." I yell at the phone. Yes, I actually do.

Me: Fine. You win. I'm calling in my first. I want you to fuck me. And it better be worth it, Spencer.

Logan: Already on my way.

Oh my gosh. Did I really just do that? Did I really just ask him to come over? Looking down, I'm still in my ugly pajamas and it's already after lunch.

Jumping in the shower, I take the fastest shower of my life. Making sure to clean all the important parts, I scrub as fast as I can.

It only takes Logan ten minutes to drive over here. If he really was already on his way, I may have less time than that. Though, I'm sure he was just saying that.

Ten minutes later, I'm throwing on the sexy bra and panties I sent him a picture of yesterday. The anticipation is making my sex buzz.

How will this go? Will we be awkward? Will it be like last time where we ease into it? Will he come barreling through the door and rip my clothes off? I'm honestly not sure which one I want more.

Just as I pull my hair into a braid, I hear knocking on my door. "Here we go." I throw on a simple dress before walking over to the door. Opening the door with shaky hands, I see my silly, cocky Logan that I have come to enjoy.

He is leaning on the doorframe as if he has been waiting there for several minutes. "The dick you ordered is here," he says with a wink. Even though we are just friends every time he winks at me I shiver.

Laughing, I shake my head. "You're a dick alright. At least I thought you were when we first met."

"And now you can't keep your hands off of me." He pushes off the doorframe and starts his way inside.

"What can I say, you're just irresistible," I joke as I let him in. Though his joking eases my nerves, they are still butterflies circling my stomach. Maybe alcohol will help.

"Want a drink?

"Sure. Don't drink too much. I don't want to have to be a good guy again and not get to have sex with you because you drank too much."

"Shut up. Even if I did drink a lot, I asked you to come here because I want to have sex with you," I say as I stick my tongue out at him. "Count yourself lucky."

"Oh I do." I see him adjust himself as he walks further into my apartment. He's trying to play it cool, but he's already hard and ready to go. I'm not sure if I should march over there and take what I want, or if I should play hard to get?

Going to the fridge, I pull out two beers. Handing one to Logan, I sit on the couch right next to him. Dragging my legs over his lap, I take a long drink of my beer, hoping it will calm the rest of my nerves.

Logan matches me as he drinks his beer. Moving his hand to my ankles, he softly runs his fingers up and down my shins. Feeling the heat pull between my legs, I relish in his touch. You'd think it would be weird having your best friend's hands on you, but it's not. It's such a normal feeling.

His hands move from my shins up to the top of my knees. He's making his way to where I want him most, but he is taking entirely too long. We both drink our beers faster as if when we finish the beer we can finish each other.

Taking one last long drink, I place my beer on the coffee table. Logan follows suit even though he hasn't finished his beer. I watch his movement, and as soon as he sits back against the cough, I crawl onto his lap. I'm tired of waiting for what I want, so I take it.

Without a word, I slid my hands up and down his chest. Feeling the strength and softness in it at the same time. Settling on the back of his neck, I pull him in for a kiss. It's soft at first, even sweet with a sense of longing.

Grinding myself against him, he reaches up and grabs the back on my neck and pulls me down harder against him. I can fully feel his length against my panties. Reaching down, I pull off my dress. I watch as he takes me in.

"These damn bra and panty sets. Of course you would wear them. You look beautiful in them, Alice. I almost jerked off to them when you sent me those pictures. I was trying to play it cool though." I'm surprised he admitted all of that, but it makes me smile.

"I'm glad you like them. I got them yesterday." I start kissing his neck, down to his collarbone. I'm tired of talking, I want him inside of me, now. Sensing my need, he slides his hand between us and starts rubbing my throbbing mound.

"As you can tell, it makes me want you even more knowing you bought these to wear for me," he says as he dips into the panties he's referring to.

The moment his hands touch my bare skin, I melt into him. He continues his torture on me as I grind into his hand over and over needing more. "Please, Logan." Granting my plea, he slips a finger inside of me. "Oh my gosh, yes."

I greedily ride his fingers, wanting more. I need it now. Grabbing the waistband of his sweats, I try to pull them down. Understanding what I want, he lifts his hips.

Removing his finger from inside of me, I pout at the loss of him. Standing up, I help him slide down his pants to his ankles.

Looking at his dick pointing straight up, I smile. That's for me. He wants me. I can tell by the way he watches me. It's not just because he is horny. Reaching behind me, I unhook my new bra and let it drop to the ground. Not waiting a beat, I slide my black, lace panties down to join my bra on the floor.

"Shit, you're gorgeous, Alice," Logan says as he kicks out of his sweats. He quickly removes his t-shirt leaving us both completely bare to each other. We watch each other for one, two, three seconds. Watching how our breathing is in sync with each other, it's a soothing sound.

Crawling back on top of him, I take him into my hand. Stroking him up and down, I search his eyes. "Condom, in my pocket." I'm glad he brought one, though I'd love to feel him bare inside of me.

Bending down, I fumble through his pockets. Finding what I'm looking for, I settle myself back against him. I hand him the packet. Thankfully, he rips it open as quickly as I want and slides it over himself.

Lining him up against my opening, I take a deep breath with anticipation. "Are you ready?" Logan rubs his hands up and down my spine. It's a sweet gesture.

"Yes, I want it now. Don't make me wait anymore, Logan." I let out a scream, as he slides inside of me before I can finish my sentence.

My head rolls back at the feel of him pushing into me. "Damn it, Alice. You feel so good." I roll my hips back and forth, up and down until we are both moaning against each other.

Taking both of my boobs into his hands, he kisses and sucks on them both. "Bite it," I tell him, and he does. "Yes, more," I moan as the pleasure makes me drunk. He continues to nibble and suck on my boobs. Feeling my orgasm build, I push down harder on him. The couch isn't allowing me to reach the spot I want.

"Take me to the bedroom. I want to feel you even deeper," I plead.

"Whatever you want, Alice." He scoots up to the edge of the couch, grabs my legs and stands up. Still inside of me, he takes me to the bed. "How do you want it?"

"I just want you deep. Now. Please." I'm having a hard time hiding my desperation.

Setting me down on the edge of the bed, he pulls one of my legs above his shoulders. I'm spread out so far, my hips feel the stretch. Knowing the pleasure I'm about to receive, I accept the twinge of pain as I stretch for him.

Starting to move slowly, he grabs my other thigh and pulls me harder against him. "Yes, that's it. Right there." His pace picks up. Faster and faster, he pumps into me. Teetering on the edge, he moves his hand between my legs and rubs my clit until I'm spilling over.

"I'm about to cum, Alice. You feel too good." I feel Logan go harder for a few more pumps and he lets out the sexiest moan as he releases himself inside of me. Moving his hand faster and faster over my clit, he continues pumping himself even after he comes down from his orgasm.

I can feel him start to soften. Seeing I'm so close, he pulls out. I almost cry out in anger, but then his tongue is on me. It takes thirty seconds before I mount his face and cum on it. Shoving two fingers inside of me, he pumps me as I ride out my orgasm.

Wiping his face, he climbs up to me and kisses my lips twice before pulling me further onto the bed. It's a good two minutes before he speaks. "Wow. That was better than I expected. We may need more than six times." I can't help but laugh and roll onto his chest.

"I guess we should have specified, if we have sex three times in one day, does that count as three or one?"

"Definitely just one," Logan answers extremely fast.

"Deal."

"Give me an hour and I'll be ready to go," he says as he kisses my temple and nuzzles into my neck.

Instead of another round of sex, we end up falling asleep in each other's arms.

Chapter 12 Logan

Most people don't know this about me, but I have a passion for photography. I do it on the side, mostly for fun. I love capturing moments of nature, the way the sun hits the horizon at that exact moment. There isn't much that takes my breath away, but that does. I've shot a few people as practice. Mainly I shot my ex before I found out she was the biggest bullshitter.

We were actually high school sweethearts. Everyone had money on us to marry right after we graduated, marry, have kids, and live happily ever after. Man, was I ever an idiot to believe that. I found out she had not only been cheating on me, but just got engaged to another guy without even telling me. Talk about a blow to my ego.

I know it's been six years since this happened, but I've never really recovered. I don't ever want to experience that again. That's why I've been living my life as cocky Logan. That is until I kissed Alice for the first time. Since that kiss, she has been all I think about. Now that I've slept with her, I don't know I'll ever get any work done ever again.

So now, I enjoy exploring beautiful lands and capturing those moments that no person can ruin. It's where I feel I'm most at peace. I'd say it's pretty out of character for me, at least that's what people say when they find out. I put on this hard exterior for people. Covering up my emotions with humor, it's a way to keep people at arms length. At least that's what my old therapist told me, but what does she know?

Then there is Alice, she has been chipping away at my walls since the moment I met her. She was just….different. She's funny, beautiful, smart, and basically everything you could ask for. The only issue is, she sees me as just a friend. Though, I'm hoping I can change that.

Taking in the view at this new trail I found behind one of the nature walks, I think about having Alice here with me. I've never wanted to bring someone on one of these hikes with me before, but I know she would make it even more enjoyable. One day, maybe.

Taking a few last shots of the setting sunset, I make my way back down to my car. Alice and I both had a pretty busy day at work today. Monday's are always the worst for all reasons. I always do updates on Mondays. Alice has to make Mr. Miller's schedule for the week, and it's just Monday.

I hate to say it, but I miss her. Even though I got to sneak several looks at her throughout the whole day, I only got to talk to her at lunch. We've started a new tradition, She always pulls our lunches out of the fridge, and I go get us both a much needed coffee. Then, we always eat lunch together. Thankfully, nothing was different today. I don't think I could bare it if it were.

I'll bide my time. I'll be who she needs me to be, for now.

Tuesday morning is the complete opposite from Monday. Both Alice and I have had a ton of time to talk. Both of the bosses had a big fancy meeting at the Corporate Tower. They will be gone most of the time, so Alice has just been fielding calls. I haven't had much going on, but I'm not complaining.

"People are going to think you're Mr. Miller's new assistant," Alice jokes as I sit on the chair I brought over.

"If anyone asks, I'm helping you with the new update. Apparently yours didn't work yesterday. So weird," I wink at her. I've noticed she loves it when I do that. Well, maybe she doesn't love it because it turns her on when I do it. Every time I wink at her, I notice she clenches her thighs together. And every time I see her do that, my dick gets hard. So really, I'm just torturing myself.

"Got it." She places two fingers against her forehead, and salutes me.

"That coffee we had at lunch isn't doing its job for me. How about you? Want to take a break and go grab some more?" Since I've spent so much time with Alice today, I've been thinking of the different ways and different places I want her spread open for me. There is one place I can't get out of my head…..here in the office.

I've been planning it out in my head since lunch. I almost locked the breakroom and called in one of my times there, but I would really hate to have someone bang on the door and get us fired. I'm thinking the closet in the kitchen would be a much better and safer place.

"Sure. I could stretch my legs." I can't help but laugh. You're about to stretch more than just your legs, Alice.

"What?" She looks at me like I'm crazy.

"Oh nothing," I say as I walk behind her. Thankfully she has on one of her infamous skirts she wears. Damn it, that's going to look so good pulled up around her waist. And there goes my dick. I feel it pushing against my briefs. It's a greedy little bastard. Apparently, my hand wasn't good enough last night. Since I've been between Alice's legs, I don't think there is any going back. I'm not sure what I'm going to do after our six times.

"It must be something," she says, turning back to look at me. Her eyes drop down to my dick that's impossible to hide right now. I need to pull it up and tuck it into my waistband, but that will be even more obvious. I'm just hoping no one comes around the corner and sees.

"Is that because of me?" Who else would it be for? Doesn't she know how beautiful she is?

"You or Mrs. Mackey. Yall both have those killer skirts on." She laughs because she knows it's from her. Mrs. Mackey is about 70 years old.

"She was looking pretty good in that coral blouse." I hear her say, but all I can think about is that I'm about to pull her panties down. I wonder if she thinks about the possibility? I wonder if she is growing wet the further we walk?

As we turn the corner, I breathe a sigh of relief. There isn't anyone in the kitchen. Shutting the door behind us, I watch her as she heads over to the coffee maker. We have a regular pot of coffee, a keurig, and an espresso machine. I'd say they treat us pretty well, and I'm about to screw Alice in here.

"Which do you want?" Alice asks as she turns around to notice I'm not following her. I'm standing by the closet that's about to see some naked butts.

"You," I admit as I start to rub my dick outside of my slacks. Her eyes go wide. Her breath starts to pick up as I continue to rub myself. Her mouth drops open. Normally I'm not one to risk my job for anything, but apparently I don't feel the same way when it comes to Alice.

"Logan, we can't."

"But we're going to. I'm calling in my first." I nod towards the closet door I just opened.

I can tell she's thinking about it. She can't refuse, that was the rules of our deal. Not that I think she'd want to refuse. I can tell she likes the idea of the risk. It's the thrill that's sparking the fire in her eyes right now. The risk of getting caught has her legs pressing together.

Her heels click quietly as she prowls towards me. The nervous Alice is gone. The excited and confident Alice brushes past me and walks into the closet.

Closing the door behind us, we don't waste time finding each other. We don't have time for teasing.

Grabbing both sides of her face, I pull her into a desperate kiss. The moment I feel her lips on me, my body takes over. I'm no longer thinking; I'm just doing.

I want to unbutton her blouse and kiss every inch of her, but we don't have time for that.

Her hands go right to my belt. Once that's undone, she hurriedly buttons me and unzips my pants. My ears are filled with our heavy breathing. My hands grab her tits and rub her nipples hard over her shirt.

Damn it, I want to feel them.

Reluctantly, I abandoned them to hike up her skirt. "Turn around." I spin her around. "Hold your skirt up." She does as I say, wanting this as much as I do.

With her skirt bunched up around her waist, I drag her panties down as fast as I can. Kicking her feet as far apart as I can with her panties still on, I slide my hand between her legs. Slipping my fingers between her folds, I let out a moan when I feel how wet she is already.

"Damn it, Alice." She moans as I circle her clit. I want to spend eternity on her, but I don't have the time right now. I'll have to make it up to her.

Inserting two fingers, I pump slowly into her. "This is going to be fast and hard. Are you ready?"

"Yes, just do it. I want it." She bends over and holds onto the shelf just below her waist.

Urgently, I pull my hardened length out and slide on a condom as fast as I can. Pushing my tip inside of her, she already starts to moan at the invasion.

Sinking all the way into her, I pause for one moment allowing her to adjust to me. Once she does, I start thrusting. Driving into her over and over as if I have a deadline, I grab her hips and pull her even closer to me.

Reaching my arm around, I roll her clit between my fingers. This earns me a delicious moan. One I want to hear over and over again. Being inside of her is where I belong. I'm sure of it, and I plan to make her realize it.

Determined to get her off with me, I bend down and angle my dick upward as I continue to roll her sweet mound. I want to roll it around on my tongue. I want to shove my tongue inside of her.

Fuck

How can I want more of her while I'm buried deep inside of her. Will I ever get enough of her?

Moving my hips faster, I feel her start to tighten. I don't stop, pounding into her I hear her cry out, "Yes. I'm going to cum, Logan." With my other hand, I grab her hand

and move it to her mouth to cover her own cries. Just as I do, her muffled screams fill the room as she comes apart.

I let go and pour myself into her. How I wish I was bare inside her. I want to feel her, skin to skin, no barriers between us.

"How do you feel so good," I say. Leaning my forehead against hers after I pull out and clean myself up.

"You're telling me. But as good as that was, we need to get out of here before someone needs extra paper or tissues," she says as she brushes her hair out with her fingers.

"Hey, those tissues came in handy," I say with a smile. I'm not sure what I would have done if they hadn't been in here. She smiles back at me as she cracks open the door.

"Okay we're good." We both quickly walk out and head over to the coffee. Awkwardly, we grab our coffee and start to walk back.

"Well, we each used one. That was definitely a fun one. One I haven't experienced before," she says, giving me a sideways smile.

"I'd have to admit, that was a first for me as well. One I'd like to do again."

Shit, did I just say that out loud?

"That was extremely fun, but we probably shouldn't risk that again. Plus, you only have two asks left." She starts walking off towards her desk on the left as I head towards the right to mine. "You better use them wisely," she says a little louder as we part ways.

Chapter 13 Alice

I've been so busy at work the rest of the week, it's been ridiculous. Apparently, my old company has been trying to broker a deal with us. They have been submitting bids for several different jobs. How weird is it going to be if I have to work with Noah. That will be the worst. I've made a good home here, and I'll be damned if I'll let him ruin it.

"I can't even tell you how happy I am that we are off tomorrow. I'm so glad that Mr. Williams was born on Valentine's day."

"Yeah, me too. I don't think I could look at a computer right now. My eyes are killing me," Logan says as he walks me to my car.

"Are you going home to sleep?" We stayed up late last night talking. We might have had phone sex. We both agreed it didn't count as a time. We were both horny, but also too tired to go over to each other's home.

I haven't done that much, but let me tell you, hearing Logan moaning over the phone was hot. It was almost like reading a book. We kept telling each other what the other was doing. We didn't video chat. He asked, but I was too nervous to do it. I told him we may next time.

"I sure am. I'm going to go take a long ass nap and then, I'll probably go for a run at my gym. What are your plans tonight?" I think for a minute. Going to my gym might be fun. I wonder if I would run into Ryder? Maybe I should just text him and see what he's up to. What would Logan think about that?

"I'm honestly not sure. It will definitely involve a lot of sleeping though. You need to leave me alone tonight. Let me catch up on some sleep so I can function," I push his shoulder a little.

He puts his arm around my shoulder. It feels normal. Not once have we been awkward with each other. We are still us, and it makes me so happy. "You know you have to come if I want to use my second time."

"I'm blocking you just for tonight. So you better not."

"Dang, I'm hurt," he slaps his hand to his heart like I shot him in the chest.

"You will survive. You still have your hand. It worked for you last night," I encourage.

"Only if I have you in my ear. If not, it's just not as fun. What can I say? I like my blonde temptress moaning." Just him saying that has me wanting to call in my second, but I'm too tired to enjoy it.

"I'm sure we can do that again. Just not tonight. I'm going to sleep for a few hours." I'm even too tired to joke with him right now, and I think he can tell.

"You good to drive?" He asks as I climb into my car.

"Yes, I'll just think about earlier in the closet. I'm sure that will keep me awake until I get home."

"Don't even start, Alice. Or I'll be climbing into that car of yours," he warns, and I believe him.

I hold up my hands as if to surrender. "I'll see you later."

"Soon, I'm sure," Logan says with a wink. Then, he strolls off to his car swaying his hips dramatically. I cannot with him. I laugh all the way home.

As soon as I enter my apartment, I go straight to my bed and crash for two hours. When I wake up, I grab one of my favorite protein shakes.

I haven't been able to get Ryder out of my head since I woke up. I wonder what he's been doing this past week? Does he think about me? Would he be interested in hanging out with me?

"Ugh," I say as I finish my shake and pour myself a glass of water. I'm being such a girl. I could just text him and find out. Taking a deep breath, I pull out my phone.

Alice: Been to the gym lately?

As soon as I send the text, my heart starts hammering into my chest. Why am I so nervous? It's just a text. I set my phone on the kitchen counter. Doing my dishes, I try to distract myself. My hands are deep inside a pan when I hear my phone buzz.

Jumping, I bump the edge of the pan and it flys to the floor. I fumble with the dish towel to clean my hands. Leaning for my phone, I trip over the rug and knock over the glass of water I was drinking from. The water goes right for my phone. "Shit. No." I run for my phone before the water can get to it.

Grabbing my phone before the water can get to it, I laugh at myself. Opening it as fast as possible, I see a text from Ryder. I let out a squeal.

Ryder: I have. But I haven't seen you there.

Alice: So you know who this is?

I look down at the mess I made, and laugh again. I can't believe I did that. Going over to clean up all the water I spilt, I hear my phone buzz again. Trying my hardest not to make another mess, I read my text.

Ryder: I haven't given my number to just anyone.

I'm not sure why, but a smile covers my face. I'm glad he hasn't been giving out his number. Unable to stop myself, I text back right away with a huge smile on my face.

Alice: Have you been to the gym today?

Ryder: Not yet, I just got off work. I'll probably head over around 9. Are you wanting to join?

Do I want to watch Ryder workout? Um, yes!

Alice: You work late. What do you do? And yes, I'd love to join.

Ryder: I'm a foreman. We work all kinds of hours.

Of course he works outside. He has those natural, sexy muscles. His tan skin and those hands are mouth watering.

Alice: So that's where your strong hands come from?

As soon as I hit send, I cover my face. I can't believe I sent that. I'm obviously referring to when he fingered me and got me off in the bathroom of the bar we met at.

Ryder: It is. Would you like to feel them again?

I squeal for the second time. This guy thrills me like I'm not used to. Not that I don't have fun with Logan, I do. I'm just at ease with him, which I love. But Ryder brings out a different part of me that I'd love to explore.

Alice: I can admit I've thought about them a time or two.

Ryder: Tell me about these times.

Oh my gosh, am I about to have phone sex with Ryder? When I did it with Logan, we were talking on the phone. I'm not sure how to do this over text.

Alice: What exactly did you want to know?

I know what he wants to know, but I can't help but feel shy. Though I shouldn't. It's not like he can see me or even hear me for that matter.

Ryder: Did you touch yourself?

I suck in a deep breath and plop down onto the couch.

Alice: I did.

His texts are coming in so fast. He must be glued to my phone like I am.

Ryder: When? Where?

Alice: The night after. In my bed.

Ryder: Did you use your fingers? Or did you use a toy?

I can't believe I'm about to admit this to him. I'm pretty sure he is pulling out the dirty side of me. Sure, I had phone sex with Logan, but it's different with him. We were friends first. I feel 100% comfortable with him. Ryder on the other hand…I'm starting to sweat over here, and he isn't even in front of me.

Alice: I used my fingers at first, but I couldn't reach the spot you did so I used my vibrator.

Ryder: Fuck that's hot. I want to watch you.

I don't text him for a minute. Watch me? Oh no. I'd be way too embarrassed to do that in front of him. He must be impatient because I get another text from him.

Ryder: Let me watch you, Alice.

Ryder: I'm hard right now thinking about you touching yourself while thinking about me.

Hot damn. This man is going to be the death of me. *Death by orgasm.* What a way to go.

Alice: I'd be way too nervous to have you watching me.

Ryder: We can work up to that. Touch yourself right now.

I jump off the couch. My new found energy is surprising.

Alice: I just pulled my pants off, now I'm on my back in my bed.

Ryder: I just unbuttoned my jeans and let them fall to the floor.

Alice: Are you touching yourself? What are you thinking about?

Ryder: My hand is wrapped around my dick. I'm pumping it slowly. I'm thinking about how wet your pussy is right now.

Ryder: Rub your clit for a minute, then shove a finger inside yourself. Send me a picture of how wet your fingers are.

I do what he says. I rub my fingers against myself. Already starting to feel that familiar build up. Shoving a finger inside of myself, I let out a moan. Usually my own fingers inside of me don't get me off, but the way Ryder is talking to me I think they just might.

Mustering up some courage, I take a picture and send it to him. He responds right away.

Ryder: God dammit Alice. I want to be the one fingering you. I want to taste your pussy. I want to know how you feel when you ride and cum all over my face.

His words are crass, but I'd be lying if I said they weren't turning me on.

Alice: Your tongue on me would send me over the edge right now.

Alice: Are you close?

Ryder: I need to see you. Either let me facetime you, or let me come over to watch.

I want him to come over and watch me, but I'm worried it wouldn't stop there. I don't really know Ryder. Plus, I'd have to talk to Logan about it first. That was part of the deal.

Ryder: Decision time.

He called me. I'm so turned on right now, I don't think. I just answer. His sexy face is on the screen. I can tell he's shirtless.

"Hello beautiful. Are you still ruining yourself?" He doesn't miss a beat. He pulls the phone away from his face, allowing me to see his bare chest and arms.

Good lord, his chest has a large eagle tattoo that covers both his pecs. There is a flag in the background. It's hot as hell. I want to run my fingers over it.

Once I get past his sexy tattoo, I slide my eyes down his torso. He clearly has a six pack. I can see that the gym has paid off very nicely.

I'm not one of those girls that have to have a guy that's ripped. I find all levels of fit attractive, but Ryder's body is divine. I can see his arm moving, and it sends heat to my core. I know he is jerking off while looking at me.

"You still with me?" He asks, breaking me from my trance.

"Yes. I was distracted by your body. It's mesmerizing," I admit as I continue to rub myself.

"You need to see it up close. Maybe run your hands down it." I can tell he is getting close. His voice is jerky.

"I'd love to run my hands all the way down. To grab that dick that's in your hand right now. Maybe put it in my mouth." I'm shocked by my words, but it's about to send him over the edge.

"Fuck, Alice. I want to see your pussy. Show me."

I pause for a moment. I've never done that before. I've never even had phone sex on facetime before.

"Alice. Please. Just show me," he pleads with me.

Instead of having the phone looking back at my opened legs, I switch the camera around so he can only see the top of where I'm touching. I continue touching myself even though I'm the most nervous as I've ever been.

"God dammit, Alice. You look so fucking hot," he says as he turns his camera around so I can see him rubbing his dick.

"Wow, good lord," I let slip out of my mouth. It's large, and It curves slightly to the right. That will be fun to play with.

Am I going to play with it?

"Cum for me, Alice. I'm not going to last much longer seeing you like that." I watch as his pulls go faster and faster.

Circling my clit over and over, I let out a loud cry as I come apart. "Oh God."

I ride my orgasm out as I watch Ryder spill all over himself. "That's all because of you, Alice." He holds up his hand and shows me all the cum that's covering his hand.

We both flip the camera back to our faces. "I can't believe I just did that. I've never facetimed like that."

"Well it was hot as hell. We need to do that again. Or better yet, do it in person." The thought of watching Ryder jerk off over on my chair in the corner while I'm on my bed touching myself has me wanting more already.

"I think I'd enjoy watching you in person," I admit to him in a soft voice.

"Good. I'll see you at 9 in the gym.

Chapter 14 Ryder

Today was one of the rough days. I've been the foreman for my company for almost four years. I've lived in OKC for most of my life. Did everything my family expected except drop out of college and get a job at my uncle's construction company. So basically, I was a screw up after high school. Hey, at least I waited until after I moved out of their house to "mess up my life" or so they say.

I'm not close with any of my family. I've never had a roommate, or lived with a girlfriend. I've always been a loner. The guys on my crew are my family, though none of them are like family.

I'm not sure that even makes sense.

I'm not sure what a girl like Alice would see in me other than my looks, but I can't say I hate the attention. The last girlfriend I had was last year. It was a mutual break up, so I wouldn't say I have any deep scars. I know I want to settle down one day and get married. I'm just not sure when that day is.

Arriving at the gym twenty minutes before nine, I start my workout. I knew I wouldn't be able to get a good workout in with her around. Especially after seeing her touching herself. I know it's all I'm going to be thinking when I see her. I was honestly surprised that she actually showed me herself, and damn it I'm glad she did. Even though the angle didn't show her off very much, it was still hot as fuck.

Watching her come apart from her own hand while thinking of me was heaven. Trying to focus on anything after that was impossible. Even though I got off, I've been bursting in my briefs at the thought of seeing her. Even now, I'm having a hard time hiding myself in these shorts.

Since I met Alice, she has filled my mind. The way her pussy felt on my fingers. The look in her eyes when I told her I wanted to help give her a release. They turned heavy and drunk on endorphins. I will never forget that hooded, aroused look.

I kept kicking myself for not getting her number, but I had to leave as soon as she got off. If I hadn't left, I would have bent her over the counter, and I gave her my word it was just about her.

The only thing I got out of my sister was her name. I can't even express how shocked I was when I saw her in the gym that night. I mean, what are the actual odds of that happening? We have 15 buildings in the complex and probably a thousand people in each building. Whatever the odds are, I'm extremely thankful they worked in my favor.

Now the only problem I have is this friend of hers that she has some kind of deal with. I didn't fully understand it. I don't like that I can't have my chance with her until she is finished with him. If they are just friends, why can't she have something with me?

No, I'm not looking for a forever thing right now, but I am extremely fascinated with her. I want her, but she has him. I don't know where that leaves me, but she seems to be interested in me too. Maybe I still have a shot.

"You started without me." I hear a sweet voice say.

Turning to meet her, I immediately smile when I see Alice. She has on a tempting sage green, skin tight yoga outfit on. It's insanely inviting. It's begging me to touch her. I want to run my hands up and down the sides of it to feel her curves. Is that why she wore it?

"I knew I'd be distracted with you around," I honestly admit as I drop my weights.

I can feel her eyes burning into my arms. She's checking out my muscles. Good, I'm glad she is because I'm having a hard time not checking her out.

"Yeah, I'm not sure I'll be able to focus much. Maybe you should stay on your side of the gym while I stay on mine." She starts to walk backwards towards the treadmill.

I'm dying for her to turn around so I can see her ass in those tight leggings. And she is going to be on the treadmill. With her tits and ass bouncing. Yeah, it was a good thing I wore my compression shorts under my athletic shorts.

"I'm almost done with my workout. Then, I'll come join you on the treadmill." If I don't wear myself out with this workout, I'm going to have too much energy not to make a move on her. I mean look at her. She is fucking gorgeous.

"Alright. I'll just be over here, by myself," she says with a little pout.

Damn it, that mouth.

I just give her a smile and grab my dumbbells. Normally, I watch the mirror when working out, but today my eyes are glued on Alice. With every rep, I see her eyes roam over my body. Soaking me in, she is enjoying the show. And I'm loving every bit of this attention. I think I'd like her eyes on me all day long.

We don't talk. We simply watch each other. Occasionally our eyes will move to focus on what we're doing, but they always drift back to each other. She had picked up speed, and she is running now. Only sparing glances at me as she runs, I decided I've lifted enough. I want to be beside her.

"How far do you usually run?" I ask her as I join in on the treadmill right beside her.

"Just as far as I can go that day. It's usually only two or three miles," she says in between breaths. I watch her as her tits bounce up and down. Unable to help myself, I lean back to check out her ass. I'm not trying to hide what I'm doing. I'm making it very obvious. I want her to know just how much I desire her.

"You look hot as fuck right now," I say as I look around to see if anyone is near us. Thankfully, there are only three other people in the gym. They are all on the other side lifting weights where I once was.

Alice is the only female in this place. For some reason, it makes me feel protective of her. I don't like the thought of her in here alone. After this, I want to tell her to let me know when she decides to come to the gym late at night. She's not going to come here alone again.

I can see the blushing cover her cheeks. It's not from her workout, it's from my words, and I love the way she reacts to me. Her hand punches the down arrow on the speed button. Slowing her speed, she keeps pace at a brisk walk. She doesn't take her eyes off of me.

"So do you," she says breathily. Is she usually this shy? For some reason, I get the feeling she is usually feisty. Do I affect her that much?

Reaching down, I remove my shirt and throw it onto the treadmill. Her jaw drops as she takes me in. I definitely take pride in myself. I'm a pretty clean eater. I run every day. I lift weights every day. I don't smoke. I rarely drink alcohol. I never drink pop. I drink a shit ton of water, and I even take my vitamins. So, I can't help but smile as Alice appreciates all the hard work I've put into myself.

Letting her take me in, I watch her eyes. They start at my pecs, probably exploring my eagle tattoo. I got it after my best friend served. Unfortunately, he didn't come home.

Dropping her eyes, she moves down to my abs. They wander over every ab until she gets to the V that I've worked so hard to have.

Unable to help myself, I slide my hand onto the small of her back. Not saying a word, I just enjoy the feel of her. Her step pauses, so I reach up to turn off her treadmill. I don't want her tripping. My hand traces under the back of her sports bra. Feeling her sweat from her workout, I drag my hand down the side of her and down to her hips.

I look up at her to see if she wants me to stop touching her, but there is only heat in her eyes. It encourages me to roam her body just a bit more. I have to remind myself that we are not alone. Though I will say, it turns me on to watch and for someone to watch me. I'm not sure if Alice is into that though?

Grabbing her hips tighter, I let my other hand grab her by the ribs just under her boob. I want to grab her tits and ass and familiarize myself with her slender body. I want to grab her and fuck her on this treadmill, but for some reason, I don't think management would be okay with that.

"Do you have any idea how badly I want to pull of every last bit of your clothing, and fuck you right here." I point to the treadmill. A little pain never hurt anyone. I myself love giving a little pain with pleasure. Her ass would be perfect to spank in bed.

"I kind of want you to do that," she whispers very softly. It's so soft, I almost miss it.

"Too bad there are people in there, and probably cameras watching us." This is my chance to see how she feels about someone watching her. "Who knows, having someone watch could be fun," I continue as I wait to see her reaction.

I don't see anything but excitement. Maybe she would enjoy it. I know I would. I'd love turning her on and making her come right in front of someone. Maybe even her little *friends with benefits*. I wonder if he would be into that. I'll need to meet him to gauge where he is at. He may really just be a friend, or he may actually be in love with her and just using this deal as a way to keep her close. Although, Alice did say she was the one that had to talk him into it.

I slide my hand over her left boob and squeeze her nipple. Her eyes close and her hands clutch the side rails of the treadmill. Thoughts of me fingering her race to my mind. I want to do that again, and damn it if I can't stop myself. I slide my hand down the front of her yoga pants.

I watch her face for her response. She doesn't try to stop me or even try to form the words to stop, so I continue. Dipping my fingers into her panties, I brush my middle finger against her clit. "Would you like someone to watch you get off, Alice?"

She is thinking I mean someone on the cameras, but I'd much rather someone be in the room watching her. The thrill of it is exciting. She doesn't answer right away. She just watches me as she bites her lips. "Answer me, Alice. Or I will stop."

"I've never done that," she answers right away.

"That wasn't my question. Would you like someone to watch you get off, Alice? Would that turn you on? Would that make your pussy wet like I'm making you wet right now?" I whisper into her ear.

I notice her breathing catch then it picks up quickly. Her eyes are wide, and her body is pressing against me. She wants her release, but I will not give it to her until she tells me what I want to hear.

"I think it would turn me on if someone watched me," she finally admits.

"I knew you would. We can take baby steps. How about you cum for me standing here while there are three other people in this room. They can't see you, but you can see them." Her head turns to look at the three guys lifting weights. Then, I insert a finger and watch her eyes roll back into her head.

She nods her head, unable to speak at this point. Inserting another finger, I step up onto her treadmill. One hand deep inside her, the other hand wrapped around her shoulders to steady her.

Pushing deeper inside of her, she lets out a small moan. "They will hear you, baby. You either have to keep quiet, or we will have an audience. You choose. Either way is fine with me." She bites her lip in response.

Rolling her clit as I pump inside of her, I can feel her starting to clench. Just as she did last time, I know she is close. Out of the corner of my eyes, I notice the people moving towards the treadmill.

"Those guys are coming closer. You better cum for me now, baby, or we are going to have an audience. I'm sure they would love seeing you grinding on my fingers," I say against her ear.

My words are her undoing. I nibble on her ear as she comes apart. She rocks out her orgasm all over my hand, and I can't help but be satisfied with her. A lot of people cannot climax under that kind of pressure, but she soared like a champ.

"Dammit, baby. That was so fucking hot. Now, I want to see you do that on my tongue," I say as I lean my forehead against hers.

"Right now?" Her eyes go wide. Before I can answer, her watch starts buzzing and she checks it. I can see her face scrunch up.

"What's wrong?"

"I'm sorry. I need to take a rain check on your tongue," she says as she kisses my cheek. That's definitely not the kind of kissing I was hoping for. She goes to step down, but I grab her waist. Pulling her against me, I take her face into my hand.

"You're not going anywhere until I get a proper kiss." Sliding my hand to the back of head, I pull her into my lips.

Mashing our lips together, I roll my tongue along her lips. The sweetest moan releases from her lips. I hear her watch buzz again, and she pulls away. Reading it, she presses her hand against my cheek. "I'm sorry, I really have to go, but I think I'll be able to make it up to you. I will text you."

With a quick peck on my lips, she runs out the door and I'm left with the biggest hard on I've ever had in my life. All I can think is she is a prize to be won, and I plan on winning.

Chapter 15 Alice

"I was drunk. It doesn't count," Logan moans a cry. He texted me twice while I was working out with Ryder. He said he was calling in his second, so I did what our deal stated, I went over. I haven't told him about Ryder yet. I know I need to because I want to have sex with Ryder. He is hot as fuck.

I was going to tell Logan last night, but he was drunk when I got to his apartment. I had a feeling he was drunk by the text I received. *com ove call in 2.* The next text confirmed it. *ples.* I wasn't sure what to expect when I got to his place, but it was pretty great actually. He lasted even longer than he usually does, which he can go for a while anyways. He gave me two amazing orgasms. By the end of the night, I absolutely felt like a slut, but I'm going with it.

He didn't remember much about us having sex last night, but he remembered enough to call me this morning around 11:00 a.m. "Oh no. It counted. You used your second," I say into the phone.

"Ugh, we should have made a rule about that."

"We did. I told you you had permission to sleep with me if I was drunk. I assumed you agreed," I laugh into the phone.

I can't help but think of Ryder's words last night. *"Would you like someone to watch you get off, Alice?"* I did like it. I think Ryder proved that pretty easily. When he told me those guys were coming over, it got me off right away. I wonder what Logan would think about it? I should tell him tonight.

"You alright, Alice?" I guess he noticed my lack of talking.

"Yes. Want to come over tonight? There is something I want to talk to you about," I say nervously. Thankfully, I don't think he notices.

"Are you already trying to call in your number 2?" He asks with a laugh. I want to say *"Yes, but I want Ryder to be there as well,"* but obviously I can't say that right now.

Is that what I want? Do I want Ryder and Logan to be there at the same time? I know lots of people have threesomes, but I think it's more common to have two women, right? Maybe I should talk to Becks about it. I guarantee she would have some advice.

"Stop, maybe tonight we can just talk." I wait for his response. If he suspects something is up, he is playing it cool.

"I'll be there at six. I'll bring subs from Freddies," I smile into the phone when I hear him say he is bringing Freddies. It's my favorite sub place.

"I'll be sure to let you in," I joke with him.

"You better if you want your sandwich," he says with his low voice. I wonder if he is thinking about doing something else other than having dinner? I'm sure he is.

"Oh I want my sandwich, and you better give it to me." I can't help but tease him.

"Oh I'll give it to you, but you have to ask for it," he says with a deep breath.

"Logan?"

"Yeah?" He asks.

"Did you just turn yourself on talking about a sandwich," I start laughing.

"Shut up. I'm hanging up and taking a nap. See you at six." He hangs up before I can say bye. He must be really tired.

Taking a deep breath, I send a text to Becks

Alice: Have you ever been intimate with two people at the same time?

She responds right away.

Becks: You have my full attention. Why are you asking this?

Becks: But no I haven't, but I know my roommate has. He used to get around.

Alice: Well, as you know, Logan and I have this deal going on....

I told Becks about our deal the other day. She thought it was a great idea. I think the only person that didn't like the idea was Ryder.

Becks: Yes.......

Alice: You remember Ryder? From the bar?

Becks: YESSSSSS

Alice: Well..... Apparently he lives in my building.

Becks: WHAT? OMG! How do you know he lives there? Did you see him?

Alice: I did. I ran into him at the gym. We were both there late one night.

Becks: When did this happen?

Alice: A few days ago.

I know she is going to be upset that I haven't talked to her about this already.

Becks: And you're just now telling me this?

Alice: I know. I'm sorry! I've been the worst.

Becks: So what does this have anything to do with a threesome?

I take a deep breath. I'm not sure why I'm nervous. It's Becks.

Alice: I've been wondering how it would be to be with both of them….at the same time.

Becks: Alice Lily Mitchell

Becks: You get it girl! I approve!

I let out the breath I didn't realize I was holding. I'm glad she thinks it's a good idea because I really want to do it. It's been consuming my thoughts since last night.

Alice: Good because I'm dying to try it. I just hope Logan agrees. I know I can trust him, and Ryder is hot as hell. I know he will be into it.

Becks: When are you going to ask Logan?

Alice: Tonight!

I send her a scared emoji.

Becks: Let me know how it goes! Don't wait days this time!

Alice: You will be the first to know after Logan and Ryder of course.

Becks: Better be!

Setting my phone down. I pour myself a second cup of coffee. I'm going to need this.

I start cleaning my entire apartment. If I'm going to have a tryst, I'd like for everything to be clean.

I'm not sure if Logan is going to agree, but if he does, I want to be prepared.

By the time 4:00 p.m. rolls around, I plop on the couch for a much needed break. With a huge glass of water in my hand, I watch a show while I rest.

Knowing I need to get up and shower, I groan as I down the rest of the water. My nerves start to rumble in my stomach as I wash my hair. I can't remember the last time I was this nervous. I think I'm this nervous because I don't want Logan to be upset with me. I don't think he will. I mean, we are just friends. The only thing I think he would be upset with is having to stop our deal. The only reason he would have to do that is if he didn't want me to have sex with Ryder. I'm hoping that us all doing it together will fix that.

Just as I'm getting out of the shower, I hear my phone buzz. Toweling off the rest of me, I put my hair in the towel and walk over to my phone. I can't help but let out a squeal when I see the text.

Ryder: Hey baby. What are you up to tonight?

The way he calls me baby makes my thighs clench together every time. I'm basically melting into a puddle of water over here.

Alice: I'm having dinner with a friend at my apartment. What are you up to?

I'm nervous about how he is going to respond. Especially since he lives just a couple of buildings over from me. Not that he knows which is actually my apartment, but I wouldn't put it past him to figure it out.

Ryder: Is it Logan?

Alice: Yes…..

Ryder: I hate that I'm jealous, Alice. I want to be the one coming over for dinner. I want to be the one having you for dessert.

My jaw drops. I can feel the buzzing in my head from his words. God, this man. He never stops turning me on. I never have to wonder what he is thinking. He is raw. He is blunt. He is hot. And dear lord I hope he can be mine soon.

Alice: I'm not going to lie…..I'd love to be dessert for you, Ryder.

Ryder: Fuck, I want to hear you say my name when I'm deep inside of you.

Oh good lord. I can't handle this man. I can't imagine how he would make me feel in bed.

Alice: You're killing me, Ryder. I have to have an important conversation in about an hour, and you are not helping my mindset right now.

Ryder: What kind of conversation are you having to have with Logan?

Ryder: Are you ending things because you want to fuck me?

Is he really that interested in sleeping with me? He is insanely sexy. I'm positive you could get any girl he wanted. So could Logan. Why are they wasting their time on me? I'm not saying I'm not a catch because I am. I'm just wondering if Ryder is genuine about wanting me? I'm sure his dick wants me, but is that all he wants?

Alice: You ready for this truth bomb I'm about to drop on you? I think it may shock you.

Ryder: I'm pretty difficult to shock. Tell me.

I take a deep breath and tell him my plan.

Alice: Yes, I want to sleep with you. I also want to sleep with Logan. The question you asked me about having someone watching me has been running through my head non-stop. I'm sure neither of you would be excited about the thought of me having sex with the other, so I'm going to ask Logan if you would be interested in all three of us spending time together.

I wait for what feels like an hour before he responds. What is he going to think? I feel like Ryder is going to be the easier of the two to convince, but what if I'm wrong? What if he doesn't want to share me, and I mess this whole thing up?

Staring at my phone, holding it in my hand, I jump when my phone buzzes.

Ryder: I'd be into that.

My smile takes over the entirety of my face. He's into it. He would do it.

Alice: Really? So if Logan says yes….. You will come over?

Ryder: If I get to have you….. or at the very least, watch you…. I'll be there.

I jump up and down in excitement. Checking my watch, I see I don't have much time to get ready.

Alice: Good. I'll let you know soon.

Ryder: Don't leave me waiting long, baby. Now that I know it's possible I get to be inside of you…. I'm not going to be a patient man.

His words send those familiar shivers down my spine.

Alice: I won't. I will ask him shortly after he gets here.

Ryder: And when is that?

Alice: 6

Ryder: Good. My dick is already hard thinking about it.

"Ughhh," I say as I close my eyes and picture Ryder sitting on my couch, dick in his hand, and watching Logan touch me. I immediately feel a wetness between my legs.

Alice: I just pictured you watching Logan touching me as you touched yourself.... now I'm wet and going to be late.

Ryder: Don't you touch that perfect pussy without me.

Alice: I won't. I have to go get ready. I'll text you soon.

Ryder: You better.

Dropping my phone onto the bed, I hurry into my closet and search for an outfit. I want to look cute, but also be comfortable. I also want to give them easy access in case this goes the way I want.

I can't help but laugh at myself. I sound so slutty, but I'm going with it. I want this, and I'm not going to feel bad about it.

Choosing a short, black, flowy, off the shoulders, long sleeve dress. It's cute, but I feel very comfortable. Plus, I think both guys will love it.

Underneath, I decided on red lace panties and no bra. If I bend over just a little, you can see the bottom of my panties. It's going to drive them crazy, and that excites me.

I quickly dry and do my hair in loose curls. Putting on just a little more makeup than I usually do, I give myself a once over just before I hear a knock on my door.

My stomach flips. Logan is here, and I can't help but get even more nervous knowing he is on the other side of the door.

Deciding to stay barefoot as it goes with the sexy housewife theme, I take a deep breath and open the door.

"Hey Logan," I say with a smile. I look him up and down. He is dressed in a plain white fitted t-shirt. I can see his broad shoulders and football build, and it looks so delicious. He is wearing my favorite athletic joggers, and I automatically start mentally drooling. I can't help my eyes from roaming down to his dick. I just love the way it looks in these sweats.

"Wow. You look great, Alice," he says as he mimics my actions of looking me up and down.

"Thank you. Now get in here. I'm starving," I say as I pull him into my apartment.

"Starving for me? Jeez girl. You just can't get enough of me, huh?" Logan jokes as he walks into the kitchen and grabs two plates. He is starting to know my place just as well as I do. I kind of like it.

"Oh you know it, Logan," I say as I come behind him and wrap my arms around his waist and slide my hands down the front of his legs.

"Alice, if you keep that up our sandwiches will get cold," Logan says as he blows out a deep breath.

"We wouldn't want our sandwiches to get cold," I say as I graze past his dick and up to his chest.

"I thought you wanted to talk about something?" He asks as he rubs my hands flat against his chest. It's extremely endearing.

"Yes, I did want to talk to you." I kiss the middle of his back as I release him.

We grab our sandwiches and head to the couch. Snuggling together, we start to eat in silence.

"Thanks for the sandwiches," I finally say after eating half of my sandwich.

Logan nods his head and smiles as he eats the last bite of his. He watches me as I finish chewing. I know he is ready to find out what I have to say. Is now the right time?

"Are you going to tell me you're done with our deal?" Logan asks before I can start speaking.

"What? No! I'm not trying to end our deal...," I pause for a moment. "I'm interested in tweaking it a bit."

He looks at me questioningly. "What does that mean?"

Shit, how do I ask this? *I met a hot guy at the bar, let him finger bang me, found out he lives in this building, let him finger bang me while other people were in the room, now I want to try it again, and I want him to join us.*

Yeah, what could go wrong with that? Taking a deep breath, I cross my fingers he accepts my proposal and doesn't run for the door.

Chapter 16 Logan

"I'm not sure how to ask this," she draws her words out.

"Just ask, Alice. There aren't many things I would say no to when it comes to you," I give her my infamous wink that I know affects her. The statement is true. I feel like I'd say yes to just about anything she asked.

What could be so difficult for her to ask me? Does she want to try something freaky because I'm definitely down for that. Or maybe she wants to use some toys. That could be fun.

Shit, maybe she is wanting to stick something up my ass. Ouch! Yup, that is my line.

"I want to bring someone in with us." She interrupts my wandering thoughts. Yeah, I wasn't expecting that.

"I wasn't expecting that," I admit. "Are you wanting to bring another girl in? Or a guy?" She smiles when I finish my question. I'm a guy so of course I'd find it hot as hell if Alice wanted another chick to go down on her in front of me. That would probably be the most beautiful sight in the world.

What if she wants a dude?

I'm not saying I'd say no, but I'm not sure how I would feel seeing another guy touching her. If I say no, will she break our deal? I don't want to lose her.

"I actually met this guy before I started at our company. I ran into him just the other day, and we hit it off." Great. So it is a guy. Why does she want this guy?

"Am I not satisfying you?" I'm immediately pissed off at myself because of the way my voice just sounded.

"Logan, you absolutely do. You do not need to be worried about that at all. I promise. To be honest, I wanted to explore things with him. But I don't want to give you up. I know our deal says that if we find someone, we need to let the other person know. Well, here I am, but I don't want you to decide to stop sleeping with me. I thought it would be fun if he joined in," she says all in one breath. It sounds like she is nervous about this.

I really want to know if she would break our deal if I said no? My curiosity gets the better of me. "If I said no, would you break our deal to pursue him?"

I see her processing. I'm not sure why she would say no? To her, we are just friends. I haven't told her how much I'm dying to take her on a real date. I want to come home with her as her boyfriend. I don't want to be a friend she calls to hook up with. I love being her friend, but I want more.

"No. I wouldn't break our deal. Our friendship is too important to me. You have become very important to me." Her admission shocks me to my core. No, she didn't say she wanted to be with me, but she said I was important to her. That's a step at least.

"That's good to know," I say with a smile. "So when would you like to have this guy over?" I ask her as I slide my hand up her thigh. I want to remind her just how good we are together.

Her body stiffens, and I see her breathing quicken. "Tonight?" She whispers. She isn't telling me. She is asking me.

Tonight? Hum. Do I want to do this? Who am I kidding…the thought of having someone watch as I get Alice off definitely turns me on. But how will it make me feel watching him fuck her?

I like to think of myself as a pretty open guy, so I'll try just about anything once. Who knows, maybe I'll enjoy it. Or maybe I'll hate it.

"Okay," I say as I continue moving my hand up further. "Did you want to text him now?" I lean down and start kissing her legs. Her dress has ridden up giving me easier access to her.

"Yes," she whispers as she goes to grab her phone. I let her get up and grab her phone that was on the coffee table. Pulling her back down to straddle me once she grabs it, I start running my hands over her amazing body. The body I'm about to share with another guy. The body that I want to be completely mine.

She sends off a text and places her phone down as she enjoys the feeling of my hands on her. I hear a moan escape her lips as I cup both of her boobs and squeeze her nipples between my fingers.

I know what you like, Alice.

"How long do we have before he gets here?" I ask right before I hear a knock on the door.

"He lives over just a few buildings," she admits with a smile.

Lucky bastard.

I expect her to get up right away and open the door, but she doesn't. Instead, she grabs both sides of my face and kisses me. She doesn't just give me a sweet kiss. She attacks my mouth with her tongue as she grinds herself on me.

I'm not sure how long we kiss, but I have to pull away because I can't breathe. Plus, her grinding felt so good, I'm ready to be deep inside of her. I guess we are about to see how this is going to go.

"You can answer it," I say as I give her another soft kiss on the lips. She smiles and slides off of me.

When she answers the door, I see him resting himself against the doorframe. We must have been kissing longer than I thought. He is dressed in jeans and a black fitted t-shirt. The outfit is paired with black tennis shoes. "Hey baby," he says as he kisses her on the cheek.

Baby?

Alice said they have only known each other since right before she started her job, but he is already calling her baby? I don't even call her that.

"Logan, this is Ryder. Ryder, meet Logan," she says as she introduces us. I stand up and shake his hand.

"Nice to meet the famous, Logan," Ryder says with a straight face. His words surprise me. She talks about me to him? That's a good sign, but why am I just now hearing about him?

"It's nice to meet you as well. Come on in," I say as if it's my apartment. I guess you could say I'm marking my territory.

"I'll get us all drinks. Logan, will you turn on some music?" Alice asks in her soft, sweet voice.

"Of course." I walk over to her laptop and turn on her favorite playlist as she brings us both a beer and two fingers of whiskey. I guess it's going to be that kind of night.

"You look fucking hot, baby," Ryder says as he takes a seat on one side of the couch. She smiles in response. I accept my glass from Alice as I take a seat on the other side of the couch. "Thanks, Alice." I just can't find it in myself to call her baby.

Alice takes a seat right beside me and motions for Ryder to come closer to her. He downs the whiskey and sets his glass on the coffee table. Then, he makes his way closer to us. His hand rests on Alice's thigh, and I can't help but watch as he rubs his finger in circles on her.

Throwing back the rest of my whiskey, I set the glass on the coffee table. Placing my arm around her on the couch, I keep watching Ryder's hand as it moves up her leg even more. The circles turn into an up and down motion, and I must admit, it's mesmerizing me.

I can feel the whiskey starting to warm my body. Before I know it, I start to mimic Ryder's movements. Starting my hand at her knee, I slowly drag it all the way up to where her legs start to form her V. I feel her body arch into my touch. Looking over at Ryder, he is watching my hand now.

Alice instinctively opens her legs for us. Ryder's hand has followed mine up to the bend of her leg and is now tracing the outline. She starts to wiggle. She wants our hands on her most delicious part. I have to admit, this is hot.

Moving her hair from her neck, Ryder starts to kiss her collarbone. Leaving a trail of kisses against her exposed shoulder, I watch as he does. Unable to help myself because I want to be the first to touch her, I move her panties to the side and ease in my fingers. Rubbing circles against her swollen mound, I hear a moan release from her lips.

As soon as I hear her moan, I feel my dick pressing against my pants. I'm already about to explode just touching her. She does something to me, and now the situation is even more intense.

Inserting one finger, I slowly rub on her favorite spot. "Oh yes," she says as she leans her head back against the couch.

"You like that don't you. You always have," I growl against her ear and she nods. Damnit, she is beautiful. Her back arches even more, trying to get me to move faster. It's not time for that yet.

"Doesn't she have the best pussy you have ever felt," Ryder says as he cups her left tit in his hand and squeezes her nipple. Her moan is even louder with him working her neck and tits as I'm finger banging her.

"She sure does. It's pure heaven when you're inside of her," I answer before I realize what he said. He must have felt her pussy before to have said that. I'm not sure how I feel about it, but I give him an evil grin. Not out of malice, but because he is about to enjoy something he will never recover from. I know she had ruined me for anyone else, and I would do it all over again.

Chapter 17 Alice

We just started and I'm already about to have the most mind blowing orgasm. The way Ryder is kissing on me and squeezing my boobs while Logan is pumping his fingers inside of me, it has my toes literally curling. I'm pretty sure I'm going to die tonight from over pleasure.

Is that even possible? I think it might be.

Ryder reaches up and yanks down my dress, exposing my boobs to both of them. I'm so turned on, I don't even feel the normal shyness I feel. Feeling Ryder rub his hand over both of my boobs, I'm pretty sure I'm having a sensory overload. This feels too good, and we have just begun.

It's as if my dreams just came true because they both lean down and pull each nipple into their mouths. I have two men sucking on my tits at the same time, and I cannot believe I'm experiencing this. How lucky am I?

Logan inserts another finger causing me to cry out from the intensity of it all. Feeling Ryder move his hand down the front of my panties, I wonder where he is going? Logan already has his fingers deep inside of me. I don't think he could fit anymore inside of me.

Surprisingly, he starts to rub my clit as Logan continues to hit my g-spot over and over. "You sound so fucking good, baby." I hear Ryder growl against my temple. It's almost as if he is in pain. Everytime Logan shoves his fingers in and out, I make a sloshing noise.

"That pussy is soaked isn't it?" Ryder turns and asks Logan. I can tell they are both very pleased with themselves already.

"Dripping," Logan says with a devious grin. I'm so glad he is enjoying this so much. I never want to stop.

With both mens lips on my nipples, Logan's fingers deep inside of me, and Ryder's fingers circling my clit, I come apart. My orgasm tears through me with a vengeance. It's almost as if it's angry it has been deprived of this kind of attention for so long.

My body convulses, and they both ride my wave with me as if they are enjoying it as much as I am. As soon as I come down, I open my eyes and see Logan and Ryder pulling their fingers out of my panties.

Sharing a look with each other, they both smile and turn back to me. Unsure of what to do next, I reach over and start rubbing both of their dicks under their pants. They are so hard, I'm wondering if they are in pain.

"Maybe you both should take these out," I say as I look back and forward between the two seductive men. Without saying a word, they both pull out their dicks. Logan slides down his joggers first, and I watch him spring out. Licking my lips, I have come to enjoy this dick. It has felt amazing inside of me. It's the perfect size, and a little wider than average. Grabbing him in my hand, my eyes close as I enjoy the heat of him. "Damnit, Alice. Even your hand feels amazing," Logan groans out between my tugs.

Then, I look at Ryder. He slowly unzips his pants as he looks between my eyes and my hand that's rubbing Logan. It's hot as hell that he is watching Logan's dick. I can already feel that familiar aching between my legs.

As soon as I see Ryder pull himself out, my mouth drops. He isn't as thick as Logan, but he is longer.

I can't wait to try that out.

Reaching over, I wrap my other hand around Ryder. "Fuck, baby. Even your hand is magical," Ryder growls as I continue my pumping. I don't know where to watch. I want to watch them both, but I can't at this angle.

Releasing them both, I stand up off the couch, turn around, and drop to my knees in the middle of them. Now that I am facing them both, I wrap my hands around each of them once again. Somehow they feel even harder than before. I want to put them in my mouth, but I can't do them both at the same time.

Seeing pre-cum glisten off both of their ridged dicks, I can't help myself. Leaning over towards Logan, I start with him. Staring up at him, I lick the head of his dick. "Shit," he slowly releases from his lips. It sounds like a tire deflating.

Looking over at Ryder, he is full of desire. His hooded eyes are daring me to lick him. I'm somewhat hesitant. Ryder is that dominant, forceful guy that would grab you and screw you against the wall if he was unable to resist you. Teasing him may make him see red, but I kind of want to make him see red. I want to see that side of him.

Starting to jerk off Logan again, I lean over and lick the tip of Ryder's swelling dick. "Fuck." Ryder sucks in the longest breath of air. Leaning away, he grabs a handful of my hair and forces me to suck on him a little longer. I never stop my movements on Logan.

I could suck both of their dicks all day long. The desire in their eyes alone would keep me going. Knowing how badly they both want me, it pushes me on. Before I can go over back to Logan, Ryder grabs me under the arms and tosses me back onto the couch. I'm sitting how I was earlier, but with my legs closed together.

Ryder reaches up and yanks down my panties in one swift motion. "It's my turn," he snarls at me. Then, he turns to Logan. "Don't you think?" For some reason it's turning me on even more the way Ryder includes Logan. It's as if he truly wants him here and it wouldn't be the same without him.

"It's really only fair," Logan shrugs his shoulders as he reaches up and brushes the hair from my face. I think Logan just got even hotter. "Don't worry, you will enjoy it," he continues. What has gotten into Logan?

Ryder shoves both of my legs up onto the couch and spreads me wide. Both guys watch as my most private part is on full display for their pleasure. "I've been dying to taste you, baby," Ryder whispers as he gets extremely close to me. He blows on my wetness, and it makes me jerk. Then he blows hot air on me, and I melt into the couch. I've never had someone do that to me before.

"She's the sweetest thing you will ever taste in your life, man," Logan growls as he steps closer to me. His dick is in my face, and I want to lick it again. Kneeling onto the couch, he offers me his dick like it's a prize.

Taking him into my mouth, I feel Ryder's hands teasing me all around my clit, but never exactly where I'm wanting it. "Please," I moan just as I'm about to lick Logan.

"Tell me what you want, Alice," Ryder demands. He isn't in the habit of asking. He usually tells you what to do. I can't say I hate it.

"I want you to lick me, please." Turning to Logan, I say, "And I want to suck you." I feel so dirty. I've never said these kinds of things in my life, and now I'm saying them to two guys at the same time.

Logan grabs the back of my head and thrusts into my mouth just as Ryder licks the center of my core. My moans are muffled by the girth that is Logan. The vibrations from my moans cause Logan to moan. "You're… so good at… sucking my dick, Alice. It's like… you've been doing it… your whole life," Logan says in between thrusts.

Logan's words cause me to suck him harder, my right hand circles the base of his shaft as I bob my head as much as I possibly can. I keep getting distracted by Ryder's tongue. He is about to make me cum for the second time tonight. I'm going to be so spent after this.

I feel Ryder pick up his pace just as Logan does. His tongue on me is relentless as he inserts two fingers in at once. After two more pumps I'm coming all over his face. Once I come down from my second roller coaster, Ryder licks me clean. "You were so fucking right, man. The sweetest," Ryder smiles up at Logan as Logan pulls out of my mouth.

"Take us to the bedroom, baby. I want to lay you down, and I want to see what that mouth of yours can do," Ryder says as he stands up and pulls off his t-shirt. He exposes his hot as hell tattoo that covers most of his chest. Even Logan notices it.

As I head into the bedroom, I hear the two guys talking behind me. I can't help but smile and wonder what they could possibly be talking about. I hope it's good. Confirming my thoughts, I hear Logan say, "That sounds perfect."

What sounds perfect?

"Pull your dress off," Ryder demands just before we reach my bedroom door. I don't even hesitate. I know if I don't, he will just do it for me. Reaching down, I pull the dress off in one swift motion. Taking it in my right hand I raise it up high and drop it for dramatic effect.

"That ass though," Logan whistles. I must say, having both of them drop dead sexy men ogling me sure has boosted my confidence. I give it a little shake for good measure.

"Get on the bed," Ryder is completely back to being serious.

"On all fours," Logan follows right after him. I guess that's what they were talking about. How they wanted me. I do as they say without a word. Crawling onto the center of the bed, I look back at them. I'm completely naked and they are mostly clothed. I'm feeling a little inferior at the moment, but maybe that's the plan.

They are both watching my backside as they slowly undress. Logan pulls off his t-shirt and tosses it on to the ground. They both step out of their shoes and remove their socks. Then, they remove their pants. Logan drops his to the ground, briefs and all. My eyes go to his thick, desirable legs. Those legs that hold up his appealing football body.

Ryder takes his time as he watches me. Instead of staying behind me, he walks over towards the top of the bed. My eyes follow him with wonderment. I can feel my limbs start to shake with adrenaline.

What are they about to do?

My eyes are on Ryder as he drops his jeans to the ground and slowly steps out of them. Instead of just leaving them there, he picks them up and folds them. Laying them on my end table, he turns back to me. His dick is still bouncing out of his navy boxers. Removing them, he does the same thing with them. Once they are nice and neat, he crawls onto the bed.

Grabbing a handful of my hair, he kneels in front of me and kisses me. His kiss is soft at first, but it quickly grows rough. It's full of need. He's tired of waiting, and so am I. I'm ready to feel both of these men inside of me.

Hearing a wrapper tear open, I feel Logan crawl up on the bed behind me. His hands roam over my body in a loving way before he shoves his dick deep inside of me. I open my mouth and release a cry. Ryder takes advantage of my open mouth and slides himself past my lips. "Fuck," both men say in unison.

Not letting me take a breath until my eyes are watering, Ryder slips out for one moment to allow me a small break. Feeling Logan ramming into me relentlessly, I feel my third orgasm trekking up quickly. These guys are breaking me in the best way possible. They are filling me up completely in a way I've never felt.

"Damn it, I'm about to cum," I hear Logan say from behind.

"Shit, me too. What is this magic you have, baby?" Ryder says. I'm assuming he is joking.

"Just wait until you feel her pussy," Logan says as he pulls out.

"I can't wait anymore. Turn around, baby. I need to be inside of you." Ryder reaches over and grabs a condom. Sliding it on impossibly fast, I quickly turn around. I must admit, I am excited to feel him as well.

Turning around, I see Logan slide off the condom and glide himself inside of my waiting mouth. In a hurry, Ryder slides into me surprisingly slowly, but that doesn't last long. Before I know it, he is attacking my sex. "God, you weren't kidding. I'm not going to last long," Ryder says between pumps.

Both guys are pumping into me in unison. Ryder reaches around and starts to rub my clit as Logan plays with my boobs. That's all it takes for me to fall over the edge again. "Alice, I'm about to cum." Logan pants. I try to nod my head, but it doesn't move much. I'm ready for them to cum. I want to feel both of them pulsing inside of me, coming because they both wanted me. And that is exactly what they do. I hear Ryder growl as he finds his release. "God, baby."

Two pumps later, Logan is coming deep into my throat. It causes me to gag as I'm not a big fan of cum, but I try to take it like a champ. We all three fall into each other's arms, completely sated, completely at ease, completely happy.

Chapter 18 Ryder

What the hell was that? I was pretty excited when I got the text from Alice letting me know that Logan agreed to tonight. I couldn't get over to her apartment fast enough. I had a feeling he was going to agree. Why would he not?

I must say, Logan was pretty cool. He flowed well with me, and I with him. He didn't try to over take anything. He didn't seem timid or upset. I guess I underestimated him. I guess that means I have more of a rival than I thought I did.

From the moment I saw her on her knees holding my dick in her hand, I knew I wanted her. She is hot as fuck. How could I not want her?

But she still has Logan. Will she give me another chance? Will I only be able to sleep with her if Logan is here? As fun as tonight was, I'd sure like to have her alone too.

Looking up at Alice, I smile. Her eyes are having a hard time staying open. The back of her head is on Logan's chest and her legs are tangled around mine. Her right hand is on Logan's left leg. Her left hand is on my chest. She is playing with the hair on my chest, and it's making my dick start to tingle.

Although I'm going to be ready to go soon, I have a feeling Alice is going to pass out soon. We wore her out, and I'm loving the way her sexy body is laid over the two of us. I could get used to this.

"How are you feeling, baby?" I ask her as I rub my thumb over her nipple. She jerks in response, and covers her boobs as she laughs.

"I'm feeling extremely satisfied and needing a nap," she says as she rolls over to cuddle me. She shoves her ass into Logan's crotch as he rolls over to hold her from behind.

"You and me both," Logan mumbles into her neck.

Looking at her and the situation I'm in, I smile. "What are you smiling at?" Alice asks me. Logan pops his head up to see what I'm smiling at.

Looking from her to Logan and back to her, I take a deep breath. "I think I speak for us both…we are yours, baby. You have ruined us for everyone else," I continue with my laugh. I'm not laughing because I'm joking or because it's actually funny. I'm laughing because I'm royally screwed. She has ruined me, and I'm okay with it.

"I'm right there with you, Ryder," Logan matches my laugh. He gets it. He absolutely gets this struggle we are both in right now.

"I'm not sure what to say? I like you both a lot. I'd like to have you both in my life, but I'm not sure what that looks like?" Alice questions, not looking either of us in the eye.

"We'll figure it out," Logan murmurs against Alice's shoulder then kisses it. "Happy Valentine's day by the way," he continues as he leans over and kisses her on the lips and rubs the side of her face. "I wouldn't want to be anywhere else."

Shit, today is Valentine's day?

"You're the sweetest, Logan. You too and neither would I," she says as she kisses him back and then looks over at me. She rubs my shoulder then leans over to give me a quick kiss.

Looking down at my watch, I see it's close to 10:00 p.m. I'm supposed to meet a few guys at our current job site to get everyone settled at 7:00 a.m., tomorrow. Thankfully, I don't need to stay all day like they will be. I guess that's a perk of being the boss.

I know I just met Logan, but I feel like we could be friends if he doesn't try to take Alice away from me. I guess if we are sharing a girl, we could share a few meals together.

"Would you two want to go have dinner at LaMoores tomorrow night? I have to work a few hours in the morning, but then I'll be free," I fill the silence that has overcome the room. It's not awkward by any means, which does surprise me.

I didn't know what to expect tonight, but I didn't expect it to go this well and have this good of a time. I definitely didn't expect to like them both so much and invite them to dinner.

Alice looks over at Logan before she answers. "I'm good with that. What about you?" She asks Logan.

"I'm in," he says a little reluctantly. It surprises me when we have been having such a good time. Does he not want to share her anymore?

"Awesome! What time works for you two?"

She looks back at Logan. "I'm pretty open. I didn't have anything planned tomorrow. How about 6?"

"Sounds good to me," Logan shrugs uninterestedly.

"Me too," I agree.

We sit in silence. I watch as Alice's eyes bob open and closed. "I should probably go. I have to get up early, but I'll make the reservation. Do you want to meet here at 5:30?" I ask Logan.

"If that's okay with you, Alice?" Logan asks as he looks at her.

She smiles and nods. "Yes, that works. Then we can all ride together. That sounds fun."

I get up and get dressed after we all agree. I turn to see them watching me. "You better stop before I get back in that bed, baby." I can feel myself growing hard again.

"I'd probably fall asleep on you," Alice says.

Smiling at her, I crawl on the bed and give her a deep kiss. Pulling myself away, I give Logan a nod and make my way out of her bedroom full of satisfying memories.

Waking up to my alarm clock, I spend extra time staring up at the ceiling. Thoughts of last night kept me awake for several hours. When I was able to sleep I dreamt about it. I dreamt about Alice's beautiful face. Her long blonde hair falling over her shoulders as I slammed into her.

Those cries that escaped her luscious lips were like crack. I need my next fix already and it hasn't even been 12 hours. I knew I was a goner from the moment she was on her knees in front of me.

When I got home last night, I showered and laid in bed for a while before I fell asleep. Knowing she was only a few buildings over was killing me. So many times I was tempted to text her and ask if I could come over.

I wanted to stay the night in her bed with her ass curled up against my dick, but I wasn't sure if she wanted me to stay. I wasn't sure if Logan wanted me to stay? I'm not even sure if he stayed?

I'm still not sure what to think of their relationship. The way he looked at her through every part of last night, I knew he was either in love with her or extremely close to it. I can't see him rushing to share Alice, but I'm hoping she won't give him a chance to say no.

Jumping out of bed, I change into my work clothes, down a protein shake, and head out the door.

Running through my list of new guys that started here yesterday. Thankfully, all of them showed back up today, and I don't have to write anyone up.

Checking the new schedule for all of the flooring to be installed, I see my closest friend, Rob. "What's up boss?

How was your Valentine's day?" He jokes because he knows I'm single.

Up until the last minute yesterday, I would have said uneventful. But thankfully, it quickly changed. "It was a great day actually," I say with a cheesy grin.

"You got some, didn't you?" Rob slaps me on the back. It makes me chuckle because we aren't in high school anymore, but apparently we are.

"Seriously dude?" I shake my head.

"At least tell me about it," Rob pleads. I'm definitely not one to kiss and tell. I was never one of those guys in the locker room talking about the chick they banged at the party the night before. I always found it disrespectful, but I guess it doesn't hurt to tell him about her.

"Well, I met her at a bar." I proceed to tell him about how we met while I was being my sister's wing man at her favorite lesbian bar. I also tell him she was being the same for her friend.

I still laugh at the memory of us both assuming the other was gay. I tell Rob about how we found out we lived in the same complex, and how she has this deal with her friend. I don't get into details though.

"I just can't get her out of my mind. She is the hottest chick I have ever seen. Her ass is out of this world, and her hair is the perfect shade of blonde. I just wish I wasn't having to fight some guy for her," I inform Rob.

I really liked Logan. If the circumstances were different, I'm sure we could be friends and find chicks to bang together. But Alice isn't just any girl. I'm not sure what it is about her, but I know there is something special.

"It sounds like you got it bad if she is holding up with another guy, and you're still wanting her," Rob says as he tilts his head at me. I left out the part where I finger banged her twice, and just had a threesome with them.

"Yeah, I think I do. I think I'm stuck wanting her, man," I admit.

I do want her. I want her so much, I'm willing to share her if that's how I can get her. If we do more of what we did last night, that works for me right now. I just want to see her on her knees for me again.

Shaking the thought out of my head, I change the subject. If I don't, I'm going to start getting hard at work, in front of a bunch of guys.

"How are Ricky and James doing on cabinets? I heard great things about them from my old boss," I chat with Rob about a couple of the new guys until it's time for me to head home. It wasn't required for me to stay long, but I stayed a few hours to help out the guys. They seem to appreciate it when I do that.

As soon as I get home, I head straight for the gym. I hate working out in our gym on Saturdays. It's always packed, but I need to get a workout in.

The gym is full of people, so it takes me longer to get through my reps than it usually does. A blonde girl catches my eye, but I'm disappointed when I realize it's not Alice. Although she is hot, my eyes linger on her a bit longer than they should. Her tits are huge, so every time she steps up on the elliptical they bounce. Just as I'm about to look away, she catches me staring.

Great.

Thankfully, she simply smiles at me. I smile back and go back to my reps. They are more difficult today. Probably because I haven't drunk enough water today. My body is used to me downing a gallon of water, so when I don't it gets pissed off at me.

Grabbing my water bottle, I drink the rest of my water. Finishing up my workout with a mile run, I start to head out of the gym when I feel someone grab my arm.

"Hey. Did you have a nice workout?" The blonde from the elliptical asks. I'm surprised she came down to talk to me.

"I did. Although, I need some more water. You finished already?" I ask as she looks like she just started.

"Not yet, but I didn't want you to leave without my number." I'm surprised by her boldness. I don't think I've ever had anyone hit on me in the gym before. I've most definitely have done my fair share of trying to pick up chicks. It's flattering.

"Well I appreciate that, but I do have a girl. Maybe we will see each other around though," I say as I start to walk off. I probably could have taken her number, but I don't want to give Alice any reason not to want to be with me.

"Ainsley Fields, that's my name. Just in case you find yourself single," she says with a wink.

"Nice to meet you. I'm Ryder. I'll definitely keep that in mind. I'll catch you later, Ainsley," I give her a head nod as I exit the gym.

I jump in the shower as soon as I cool off from my workout. It's a very cold day, and the walk back to my building helped.

Our complex has the main office building in the middle. The pool, gym, theater, game room, and business room are all inside the main building. We also have an outdoor pool. All 13 buildings face the main office. So it's basically one big circle.

I can't get Alice out of my head. I wonder if she has been thinking about me as much as I have been thinking about her? It's not like me to spend hours thinking about a girl. Even with my last girlfriend, we were together for three years before we broke up. It was an amicable split, but I didn't even think about her as much as I do Alice. That has to say something, right?

I'm pretty surprised how much that girl from the gym looked like Alice. She was Alice 2.0. I can't help but laugh at myself for being ridiculous.

Thinking about dinner, I can't help but get excited. The food there is delicious. I've taken a couple of dates there, but this date is going to be extremely different. Not only is it Alice, but it's also Logan. If I'm dating Logan, and she is dating us both, does that mean we will date each other separately or always together?

I'm definitely not into guys, but I will say last night was hot. Maybe I could get used to being in a relationship with a girl and a guy. It could work. Logan and I will just be good friends who fuck Alice, our girlfriend. I've heard of weirder things. I'm open to it, I just hope she is. I mean, she definitely seemed to enjoy herself last night.

LaMoores is a pretty fancy restaurant. You don't have to wear a suit and tie, but a lot of guys do. I think I'll just go with a nice button up. Ties aren't really my thing. Sliding on my burgundy fitted dress shirt, I roll the sleeves up after I button up. Pairing it with my black slacks and black loafers, I quickly look myself over. I have to admit, I clean up pretty nicely.

Chapter 19 Alice

What am I going to do? Am I really going to date two different men at the same time? Am I going to be sleeping with them both? Together? Separately? Are we going to be in a throuple? I can't imagine what my family would think about that. I mean, we aren't the closest family, but I know they wouldn't approve. Not that I care what they think, but I'm not even sure what I think about this?

After Ryder left yesterday, Logan and I talked for only a few minutes before we got dressed. I offered to let him stay, but he said he had to do laundry and go workout. It kind of surprised me that he didn't want to stay the night. I'm wondering if he feels like we can only be together if Ryder is around because that would be ridiculous.

Logan and I were friends before all of this, and I want us to stay friends no matter what. I sure hope he feels the same way. If he didn't, I'm not sure what I would do? Logan has become such an important part of my life in the past three months. It's crazy how close we have become.

Today, I've been the definition of extremely lazy. I've watched two movies in bed, and I still haven't taken a shower even though it's almost 3:00 p.m. Sometimes I love these kinds of days, and sometimes I want my days to be packed full. It probably doesn't help that the weather is so doom and gloom.

I don't mind when the sun isn't shining, but I want to be home snuggled in bed when it's like that. I'm tempted to just ask Ryder and Logan over to my place, but I feel bad since Ryder went through the trouble of making reservations.

Ryder texted me earlier letting me know the reservations were made and the dress code for the place. He also wanted to let me know that he was going to be dressed to kill. I can only imagine how hot he is going to look in fancy clothes. Not that Logan isn't going to look just as hot, but I see Logan dressed that way all the time. And he catches my eye every day I'm at work. I've never seen Ryder dressed in fancy clothes. I'm excited to.

I've been meaning to call Becks and tell her about everything that's been going on. She's going to kill me for not calling her right afterwards.

Grabbing my phone off the bed beside me, I click on Becks' contact. She picks up on the second ring.

"Hello beautiful girl," she says with a way more cheerful voice than I have.

"How are you so cheerful with this doom and gloom weather?"

"It's just who I am," she jokes. "So tell me."

"Tell you what?" How does she know I have something to tell her?

"You've had this deal with Logan, you met this super sexy guy, and you asked me about a threesome…I know you have something to tell me." Well I guess it will be easier to tell her if she basically already knows.

I proceed to tell her about Ryder and Logan meeting and about our fun night. "Wow. If I were into guys…I would be jealous. That sounds like a hell of a time, Alice," Becks says with a sign.

"Girl, it was amazing. I want to do it again, but I'm honestly not sure what's going to happen? Logan seemed fine with it. Although, he did leave pretty quickly afterwards. I know Ryder is open to it, but am I? Like how would I even do this, Becks?"

"First off, breath. Secondly, do you want them both? Do they both make you happy individually? Would that make you happy to have them both in your life?" Becks rattles off the questions. I answer each of them in my head.

Breath. Yes, I want them. Yes, they both make me happy. Yes, I want them both in my life.

"Actually, yes," I admit to her. I really like each of them differently. Logan has been there for me, he is such a great friend. He's someone I can count on to joke around with, and he always makes me laugh. Plus, he is pretty easy on the eyes. Ryder is a conundrum to me. He is pretty quiet until he is ready to tell you what he wants. He has a big dominant side, which I love. He is sweet when he wants to be, and of course he is hot as hell. They are both my guys. I want them both. Is that wrong?

"Then do you, boo boo," Becks says, making me laugh. "Do what makes you happy, and don't ever apologize for it."

"I just love you. You always know what to say to make me feel better," I say in a swooning voice because I never know how to be serious.

"Always." I tell her about our dinner tonight and what I plan to wear. I'm still trying to decide between the emerald green dress that has a slip all the way up to my hip, or the royal blue dress that basically doesn't have a back to it. They are both floor length and sexy as hell.

"Definitely go with the emerald green. They won't be able to keep their hands off of you," Becks squeals.

The thought of them both having their hands on me again has my legs squeezing together. I don't know what it is about them together, but it's like I burst into flames.

"I like the sound of that. I'll send you a picture of the final look. I better go shower. I'm still in my pajamas," I laugh into the phone.

"Alice! It's 4:00 p.m. What time are they going to arrive at your place?" She questioned.

"At 5:30 p.m. I still have an hour and a half, but yeah, I should hurry. Bye. Love you." I hang up just as I hear her say bye.

Crap, I can't believe I waited this late. What if Ryder or Logan come over early for a pre-dessert? I run to the shower, not wasting any time.

After fifteen minutes, I'm out of the shower and immediately start to dry my hair.

Why did I wait so long to get ready?

Drying my hair as I stand naked, because I always get too hot, I do my best to dry it straight. Once I've slightly curled my hair to give it that 50s vibe, I put on my make up a little heavier than usual. Doing my best to perfect the smoky eyes, I smear on the prettiest shade of red lipstick.

It's 5:20 p.m. by the time I pull on my knee highs and sexy red teddy I ordered online. I'm just hoping the guys will get to see me in this.

Just as I finish snapping the runners on, I hear a knock at my door. Someone is early. Deciding not to cover myself in my robe, I make my way to the front door. I check the peephole before opening it. I'd really hate for it to be the older lady down the hall. I'd probably give her a heart attack as she clutched her pearls.

Smiling, I open the door. Standing in front of me, in black slacks and a burgundy button down long sleeves is Ryder. His eyes go wide when he sees me, but I'm too busy watching him to notice anything more.

His sleeves are rolled up to his elbows like he is about to do some work.

Please do some work on me.

The shirt is fitted, showing off every glorious muscle in his torso.

God help me.

"Fuck, baby. You can't answer the door like that. Not when I don't have time to bend you over that couch and have my way with you," Ryder says as he grabs my waist and pulls me to him.

"You can touch, but no touching the face or hair." I smile up at him. "It took me entirely too long to make this happen," I say as I gesture at myself.

"You look fucking sexy as hell. How am I not supposed to kiss you?" He asks as he rubs his hands up and down my sides and cups my ass.

My pulse starts to quicken as he runs his right hand over my boob. "Ryder," I say breathlessly. "We will be late to dinner if we start this." I'm about to tell him to cancel dinner when I see my door push open.

Logan walks in as Ryder is kissing my neck. I instinctively pull back a little to see him watching. The look he gives me is unnerving. It seems like he is upset, but why? Why do I feel like I've just been caught doing something wrong?

Chapter 20 Logan

Walking up the steps of Alice's apartment building, I've come to be completely at home here. It's like my second home now. Honestly, I'd rather be here with her than at my own apartment.

Reaching her door, I see it's already open a little. For a split second, worry floods me. Taking a closer step, I slowly push the door open. When I take a step inside her apartment, my worry changes to something else. Where worry once was, jealousy and anger take its place.

I've never been a jealous guy before, but the moment I see Ryder's hands on her tits and his lips on her neck, I see red. I see red, and not in the good way. She looks hot as hell in that outfit, but all I can see are his hands on her. If I had walked in and seen her like this, my hands and lips would be on her as well. I don't blame the guy, but I also hate it.

I was open to a one time thing with us all. I put on a brave face, and I made the best of it. It honestly was enjoyable if I didn't think too hard about the other guy in the room. I did it for her, for us.

I didn't think we would be having dinner together though. I didn't think that meant it was fair game for him to grope Alice like this, especially when I'm not here. It feels disrespectful to me, but maybe I misread the situation. I'm not going to lie, I have a problem with it.

The moment her eyes meet mine, she pushes him away. I don't like the way she does this. It's as if she feels she was doing something wrong. If she feels guilty that I caught her, then why is she doing it?

"Logan, you're here," Alice breaks her embrace with Ryder and comes over to give me a hug. It's impossible for me not to feel something when she does. Is it pride? Victory? Or am I just extremely turned on from the way she looks in that outfit?

Her hands fall from around my neck and rest on my chest. Her eyes inspect me. Taking me in, she smiles. I'm assuming she is admiring my suit I'm wearing. I went for high-class tonight. Though I know it's not required to wear a suit and tie at this restaurant, I knew a lot of people did. When we had my friends' engagement dinner here last year, I was surprised how classy it was. Let's just say, I wanted to impress.

The suit I picked is a solid gray, fitted suit. I don't button the jacket though. Instead, I let it fall open to show off the dark green button down long sleeve underneath. I settled on a Langsford extra thin tie which is a little more fancy than my usual attire. Though I don't wear suits very often, I must say this one was made perfectly for me.

"I'm here, and you are not dressed," I say as I lean down to her ear. "Not that I'm complaining." She slaps my chest and shimmies out of my grasp.

"You boys look amazing. I better go slip my dress on before I start peeling off each of your clothes," she says with a smile as she looks us both up and down.

"I'm sorry, I don't see the problem with that," Ryder quickly says.

Although I'd love to be balls deep inside of Alice right now, I'm not sure I can share her again. I want her to be mine and only mine. If I didn't feel the way I feel about her, I wouldn't mind sharing her. But Alice is different. She is everything to me, and I don't want to lose her. But I can't share her. She is too important to me.

Instead of replying, I simply smile at her and let her walk into her room. Once we are alone, I face Ryder. He is a little shorter than I am. He also has a more slender build than I do, but he is full of muscle. I on the other hand have a body built for football, which is why I played in college as well. I can't help but size him up. I'd like to think I could take him, but he has that ex-marine's vibe. It would definitely be a good fight.

"I don't want to ruin the night, but I have to tell you, I'm not interested in continuing to share Alice," I admit to Ryder. His shoulders square up to me. It's not in a fighting stance, but he is about to defend himself for her.

"I thought things were going pretty well. Why the change of heart?" Ryder asks calmly.

"I wanted to give her what she wanted. Yes, it was a great time, and no, I don't regret it. But I am not trying to be in a throuple. She means too much to me to be okay with sharing her." I'm honestly surprised I'm telling him this, but I want to get him to understand. This isn't happening.

"Well, I don't think this is up to you," Ryder says with a shrug. Wow. So this is how it's going to go? He isn't going to bow out. "Plus, aren't you two just friends?"

His words are like a punch to my gut. Did she tell him that? Have I misread this whole situation? Does she still only think of me as a friend? Would she not be interested in more? I felt like we had grown even closer. Maybe I'm wrong. Maybe she wants Ryder.

"We are friends, but we are also more than friends."

"Look, I'm really into Alice. She is the hottest girl I have ever met. Plus, she's different. I'm not walking away unless she wants me to," Ryder says with a shrug. I mean, I can't really blame him for that. She is different, but I don't like that he only comments on her looks. She is so much more than just a pretty face.

She is by far the funniest girl out there. Everytime we are together, I end up laughing. She's the one person that can always put a smile on my face, and that means a lot. She is the kindest person I know. She's probably kind to a fault. She's someone that takes care of others before herself. If she knew I wasn't into sharing her, I don't think she ever would have asked me to let Ryder join us.

Just as I'm about to tell him to go to hell, Alice walks out of the bedroom. Our heads snap in her direction. She is a force that pulls us to her, and we can't do anything to stop it, not that we'd ever want to stop it. We are both taken aback. I can feel the aching in my chest. She is too beautiful. She is wearing a silk emerald green gown that has the most tempting slit in it. The more she moves, the higher the slit goes. It's a tank top style that has ruching, making it even more elegant on her beautiful, olive skin. She pairs it with black high heels, giving her a couple more inches. She is a vision, and I can't remember how to speak.

"Well punch me in the dick and fuck me sideways. You look hot, baby," Ryder says as he walks up to her. Grabbing her hand he spins her around allowing us a full view of her knockout dress.

The back of the dress falls into a V, just like the front of her dress. It's sexy without showing too much, but it shows it in all the right places to make you want more. She smiles up at Ryder. "Thank you, I think." She laughs at his ridiculous comment.

"Trust me, it's a complement," he follows up. She smiles then looks over at me. I'm still having a hard time forming words that would be sufficient for her right now.

"You going to be okay, Logan?" Alice asks me with a smirk. I guess she understands my silence because she just grins at me.

I nod as I continue to look at her in awe. "You are just… breathtaking," I finally say. I usually always have some sort of smart remark to make, but not tonight. Tonight, Alice deserves my full attention. She deserves for me to show her how much I appreciate her.

"Thank you," she says with the most innocent smile. Like she didn't just almost give us both a heart attack and smile about it.

Looking down at my watch, I see it's 5:40 p.m. I mapped it before I left my apartment. It showed it would take us about fifteen minutes to get to the restaurant. "We should probably go. We don't want to be late," I say as I place my hand on the small of her back to lead her out.

"Are we good with taking my Audi?" I ask. I know Alice has been wanting to ride in it since I got it last week.

"Yes! Please! Let's take it," Alice claps her hands together in excitement.

"Good idea. My truck is all dirty from my work site. We wouldn't want to get you all dirty in this pretty little dress." Ryders innuendo is not lost on either one of us. But the kicker is, he looks at me right after he says this.

Was that a challenge? Son of a bitch.

We make our way to my car which is parked pretty far from the building. I'm trying to avoid all cars so no one hits it.

"Stay here. I will go get the car so you don't have to walk that much in those heels," I say to Alice. I couldn't care less if Ryder has to walk. I really don't like the idea of leaving Alice alone with Ryder, but I'm not going to make her walk that far.

Pulling the car up to the curb, I start to jump out to open the door for her, but Ryder beats me to it. Is this how it's going to go? Both of us fighting for Allice's attention until she picks one of us.

Although, I'm sure in Alice's mind, things are going great with our throuple. I will definitely be having a conversation with her later on.

Alice slides into the passenger side. At least she is up front with me. The close proximity of the car has me dying to touch her, so I do. Sliding my hand over her thigh, I give her a squeeze. The heat from her leg has me craving to slide my hand between her legs. It would already be there if we were alone, but I don't want to be sexual in front of Ryder again. That will just give him an invitation.

Keeping my hand on her thigh, she eventually grabs my hand and holds it. Ryder has settled into the seat, so he can't see our hands. Unable to stop myself, I slide my hand into the high slit. It reaches just below her panties, and I about explode when I see thigh highs.

Keeping a straight face, I focus on the road. Again, I don't want Ryder to see. I don't touch where I truly want to. Instead, I simply tease her. Running my fingers along the bend of her leg. Being this close to her core has me shaking with desire.

She bites her lip as I slip one finger under her panties. Thankfully, she keeps quiet.

"Have either of you been to LaMoore before?" Ryder asks. Alice doesn't answer. I'm guessing she is too distracted.

"I have once for an engagement party. It was really nice. I'm looking forward to trying something new," I respond. My focus is on the girl that just spread her legs wider for me. I sure hope what I said to Ryder made sense.

"I haven't," Alice finally says. Poor thing, she is basically panting, and I haven't even touched her sweet spot yet.

"I'm excited to show it to you, baby." There he goes again with that pet name. As soon as I hear it, I slip a finger inside of her. If anyone is giving out pet names to Alice, it should be me.

She covers her mouth with her other hand to hide her moan. I'm not mad at her, but I want to take out my anger for Ryder on her pussy. I'm not sure what's gotten into me, but I'm feeling very territorial.

Giving her a few more pumps, I have to slide out of her. We have reached the restaurant, and I don't want her on display for anyone but me. I pull up to the valet parking just as Alice covers herself back up.

Ryder jumps out and opens the car door for her. Reaching her hand out to her, she takes it with a flushed smile. I'm pretty sure he notices because he gives me a knowing stare. Letting Alice take a step ahead of us, Ryder turns to me. "I'm not dumb. I know you were finger fucking her in the car. The only difference is, I'm not jealous, but I will take what I deserve." He hurries up to Alice as his words catch up to my brain.

That was most definitely a challenge, maybe even a threat. I'm not afraid to fight for what I want. Sure Ryder is a great guy, even though I'm ready to punch him. He is fighting for what he wants, just the same as I am.

Let the better man win.

We are seated at our table right away. It has a beautiful view of the city. I wonder if Ryder has some connections to the restaurant. It's probably one of the best seats here.

"Oh my goodness. Look at this view. Thank you Ryder for getting us these reservations. It's perfect," Alice swoons as she takes in the city.

"Anything for you, baby," Ryder says as he kisses her check.

We all slide into the booth. It's a very unique table. It's very private on one side while it looks out to the city on the other. It's meant for a couple to have privacy, but there is room for all three of us.

Alice is in the middle of us, of course. Ryder is on the left of her, and I'm on the right. Seeing Ryder rest his hand on her thigh, I tense up. He is on the side of her where her huge slit is. I can feel my pulse pick up. I'm overcome with this rage. I have to continuously tell myself not to shove his hand off. If Alice didn't want it there, she would remove it.

The waiter brings us all champagne. Ryder must have ordered it beforehand. Raising up his glass, he looks over at Alice. "Baby, I just want to toast to you. Even though we haven't known each other long, I'm drawn to you like a moth to a flame. You have me completely, and I hope that doesn't change," Ryder says as he shoots daggers at me. Then, he clinks our glasses and pulls his focus back to Alice.

After we place our order, we are left alone. Feeling the slight buzz of heat from the champagne, I try my best to relax. "Are you enjoying yourself, Alice?" I lean into her as I place my arm around her. I graze Ryder's shoulder as I do.

"I really am. Thank you for being here," she says, looking up into my eyes. I'm lost in her for a moment. Her and I are all that matter right now. Seeing that tenderness in her eyes, I want to grab her and kiss her. It's as if everyone else has faded away. That is until Ryder decides to slide his hand under her slit. Pulling her focus from me to him, she watches as his hand mimics mine. He trails his fingers up her thigh just as mine did when we were in the car, and I'm cursing him for it.

She watches him as he continues his tease, just as I had. Running his fingers from the middle of her thigh up to the apex of her leg, she takes in a deep breath. I can see her chest starting to rise and fall with the movement of his hands. I can't help but feel betrayed. She wants him just as much as she wants me. He affects her body just as much as I do. I thought I was different. I thought we were different. I thought we had something special. It turns out, so do they.

I want to leave. I cannot watch Ryder touch what I want so badly to be mine and only mine.

What the hell am I doing here?

Just as I'm about to leave, the waiter comes back over to refill our glasses. Ryder doesn't pull away, but he does pause. Reaching for my glass, I down half of it. I remind myself not to drink too much since I have to drive us home.

"Thank you," I say to the waiter, but Ryder ignores them. He is only focused on Alice right now.

Leaning over, Ryder whispers into Alice's ear. She nods and giggles. I will admit, I love that sound coming from her lips, but I hate that he is the one that put it there. I want to be the reason she smiles. I want to be the reason she laughs. I want to be the reason she comes.

Ryder's fingers dip into her panties, and I go rigid. Alice must feel it because she reaches up, grabs my neck, and pulls my lips down on her. The moment our lips connect, I'm lost once again. Instinctively, I side my hand into her hair. Trying my best not to mess up her well maintained curls, I slide my hand under her hair.

Deepening the kiss, I grab her jaw and tilt her neck up even further. Just as I'm about to kiss her neck, Ryder's lips smooth over her. Did he really think I was exposing her neck for him? After everything we talked about.

Trying to focus on Alice, I continue our kiss. Hearing a moan release from her lips, I can't help but wonder. Was that moan for me? Or for him? Was she moaning because she is enjoying our kiss, or is it because he just slipped his finger inside of her?

She reaches for my dick that is slightly hard and starts to rub it through my pants. Of course she still makes me hard even though I'm seething with anger. If we were alone right now, I'd probably bend her over, smack her ass, and slam my dick into her until she was crying out my name for letting another man touch her. I've never really felt this way about anyone, but it's the rage I'm feeling as I watch Ryder finger bang Alice.

Her legs are opened wide for him. If someone came around the booth, they would get a clear view of what Ryder is doing to her. I wouldn't have as much of an issue with someone watching me and Alice as opposed to someone else touching Alice.

Breaking our kiss once again, I see she isn't only rubbing my dick, but she is rubbing Ryder's. I can't help but pause as I hear Alice let out a moan. She tries to muffle the sound by biting her lip. Ryder pulls out an explosive orgasm from her. My orgasm that I was working on in the car. The orgasm that should come from my hands just came from his. And I cannot deal.

Pushing her hand away, I move over just a little. Leaning over the table, I take in a few deep breaths. "Just a second," I hear Alice say. She places a hand on Ryder's chest to signal her pleas.

"What's wrong, Logan?" Alice asks as she places a hand on my back.

"I can't do this, Alice." I take a deep breath. Not caring what Ryder is doing. I try to focus on my breathing. I'm the most angry I have ever been, but it's not at her. It's not her fault. I'm angry at the situation. I never should have let it get this far.

"You can't do what?"

Turning my head just a little to look at her, I give her a half smile. I'm thankful her head blocks my view of Ryder so it feels like we have privacy. "This," I say as I wave a hand in a circle gesturing to all three of us. "I don't want to share you," I finally admit.

"Share me? Me being with Ryder bothers you?" She asks, lowering her voice even more.

"Can we step out and talk about this real fast?" I seriously don't want to be having this conversation in front of everyone. I especially don't want to be confessing my feelings for Alice in front of Ryder.

She nods and starts following me. "We will be right back. I'm sorry," she says as she leans over and gives Ryder a kiss. Thankfully, he says nothing.

Once we get to a private hall, I turn to her and kiss her. Pulling her against my body, I run my right hand down to her ass and grind her pelvis against me. A moan releases from my lips as my dick starts to grow hard.

Breaking the kiss after a few minutes, I look into her longing eyes. "This is how it should be, Alice. Just you and me."

"Are you saying you want to be more than friends?"

I can't help but laugh. "Of course I do. The moment I kissed you for the first time, I was addicted. I didn't know it was so deep until recently, but I want you Alice. I want all of you. I want your flaws and your bad days. I want your simple self and your messy hair days. I want your morning breath and your unshaved legs. I want to be the one that wakes up to you. I want to be the one that takes you to bed. I don't want to share you. I won't share you. I can't."

I watch her reaction. I see the moment she realizes I'm being serious. That I want her, and she is in shock.

"I mean, I want you too, Logan. I didn't realize you wanted me that way. I definitely didn't realize you felt that serious about me. I'm not sure what to do?"

"Come home with me. Tell Ryder you have to go. Let me show you just how much I feel for you," I say as I tilt her head up to mine. Her lips are just a centimeter away. I want to kiss her again, but I need to know her answer.

"I can't just leave Ryder. That would be extremely rude," she says in a whisper against my lips.

"Forget Ryder," I say, a little more irritated than I meant. "Do you want him?"

She thinks for a moment. Eyes wide with uncertainty. "I mean, I want to see where it goes." Her words stab me in the chest. I can physically feel my heart breaking as she utters those words.

"Do you want me?" My words come out in a whisper. I start to repeat myself because there is no way she heard me, but she nods her head.

"I do."

"So you just want us both then?" I can't handle this. I can't let her be with another guy when she is with me.

"Realistically, I know I can't have you both in the long run, but I just thought we were having fun right now. I wasn't looking for a serious relationship, Logan." And again, she pushes the proverbial knife further into my chest.

"Well I can't. If you don't choose me, then you're choosing him," I say with pleading eyes. Please, don't choose him. Choose me. Love me. Be with me. I can make you happy.

Her silence is my answer. It's the twisting of the knife as it pierces my heart and leaves me for dead. You might as well put a *do not resuscitate* sign on my chest.

"Are you able to find a way home? You have the Uber app on the phone, right?" I ask her because there is no way I'm leaving her stranded. If she doesn't, I'll call for one myself.

"I do, but I don't want you to leave, Logan." Her plea is half hearted. I know she means it. I know she values our friendship, but we are both at a loss. And she knows it's best if I go.

"Take care of yourself, Alice. I'll see you at work," I say as I hand her a fifty dollar bill. I don't want her paying for my meal. I also don't want her to be stranded just in case.

She doesn't say anything. She just looks down at the money I placed in her hand. Without saying another word, I walk out of the restaurant dragging my broken heart.

Handing my ticket to the valet, he takes off to get my car. "Logan!" I hear Alice calling my name. Jogging back to her so she doesn't have to walk far in her heels, I can't help but smile.

Maybe she changed her mind. Maybe she is choosing me. "What is it, Alice?"

"Why is this so important to you? I know you want to be more than friends, and we can be. I just don't see why we can't hang out with Ryder also? Why are you being so difficult?"

Difficult?

"You think I'm being difficult because I want you to myself?" I can't believe she just said that.

"Well, yeah. What other reason could there be? We had a great thing going and you're ruining it," she starts to raise her voice.

I feel the words about to come out of me like vomit. I can't hold them in any longer. Before I know it, I'm spilling my heart out to the woman that means everything to me.

"It's because I freaking love you, Alice. From the day I kissed you I fell. And I didn't just fall. I fell hard. I'm in love with you!" This is the first time I've even admitted this to myself, but I'm not surprised.

Alice stands there in shock. Not saying a word. Her face says it all though, and I'm not sticking around to hear her say she doesn't feel the same. "Don't worry about it. Forget I said anything. Enjoy your evening, Alice."

Taking the keys from the valet, I hop in my car and drive off with my broken heart in tow.

Chapter 21 Alice

Standing there in the cold, I watch Logan get into his car. He pulls out of the restaurant so fast, his tires screech. He loves me? He loves me? And then he tried to take it back? Why didn't he tell me sooner if he really does love me? I wasn't meaning for this to happen. I didn't want anything serious. We weren't supposed to let our feelings get in the way of our friendship.

Should I have begged him to stay? Maybe? But he shouldn't have left me here. I honestly thought things were going well between the three of us. I was excited for our new adventure with Ryder. I wanted Logan with me as I explored him.

I'm angry with Logan for leaving me. I also have conflicting feelings about what he told me. I don't understand why he couldn't have just given this a chance. You'd think if he loved me he would be willing to wait for me. But he didn't. He just gave up.

"Whatever," I say to no one, completely pissed off. If he doesn't want to stick around, fine. Heading back inside, I see Ryder's worried face.

What am I going to tell him?

Walking back to our booth, I slide in next to Ryder. "Where is Logan?" He asks.

"He left. He said he couldn't do this anymore," I say as I gesture between the two of us. I'm angry, but I try not to show it.

"I'm sorry, baby. I know he was your friend," Ryder says as he kisses the side of my head.

He was more than my friend.

I surprise myself when I think this. I guess somewhere between all the lines, I caught feelings, but he walked away. He is much more to me than just my friend, but so is Ryder. I want to see where things can go with him. He makes me feel excited. I'm always wondering what's next when I'm with Ryder.

Our food arrives just in time. I know I'm hungry, but my stomach is in knots. Picking around my lasagna, I try my best to be in a good mood. It's not Ryder's fault Logan decided to bail. I have an amazing guy right next to me I get to focus on.

"How's your food?" I ask after a few bites. Ryder ordered the chicken alfredo, and it looks amazing.

"It's probably the best alfredo I've ever had. Would you like a bite?"

Ryder and I talk like normal for what feels like forever. I will say I miss Logan, but it is nice having some one on one time with him that isn't just about sex. Although, I am starting to feel the desire to take him to bed. This champagne is getting to me, but I'm enjoying our conversation.

We talk a little about Logan, and what my thoughts are about it. I admit to him that I'm a little sad about him leaving. I also inform him that I wouldn't want to make him uncomfortable. I decide to leave out the part about him telling me he loves me.

Logan ordered the lasagna as well, so I box it up with the rest of mine and plan to take it home. Maybe I can take it to him and see how he is doing? Though I should really be mad at him for leaving me, I can't help but worry about him.

Ryder leads me outside as we steal kisses between steps. We are both a little tipsy, and everything is funny right now. We order an Uber and slide into the back of the SUV. Turning and putting my legs on Ryder, I nuzzle into his neck. Taking a deep breath, I smell his old spice cologne and melt. I love his smell. Unable to help myself, I start kissing his neck.

"You're playing with fire, baby. Do you want to get burned?" His question is surprising to me, but it turns me on. I love this side of Ryder. The dark and dangerous side is alluring. It draws me in and holds me captive until I am no longer in control of myself.

The old Alice would never crawl onto a guy's lap in front of our Uber driver. We are so getting a zero star review. I giggle at the thought, but I don't care at this moment. I don't care about the fight I just had with Logan. I don't care about the fact we might have messed up our amazing friendship. All I care about right now is being here with Ryder.

The alcohol has consumed me now. My head spins as Ryder slides his hands up the back of my dress. It could just be Ryder too. The way he makes me feel is intoxicating.

Kissing on his neck, I grind myself against him. I can already feel him growing harder against me. Trailing kisses from his neck up to behind his ear, I wrap my arms around him and find his lips again.

I think the driver says something, but I don't even waste my energy looking up.

"Baby," Ryder says, breaking away from our kiss. His breathing is ragged and he is completely hard now. Realizing I haven't answered his question, I smile and evil smile.

"Yes, I want to get burnt. Burn me to the fucking ground. Burn me until I'm nothing but ashes, Ryder!" I want to experience this thing to the fullest. I don't want to hold back, not if I'm going to make a choice.

A choice? Did I say that? Am I choosing between Ryder and Logan?

Shaking my head, I try to throw thoughts of Logan out the door. Ryder didn't leave me. Ryder is here.

"Damnit, baby. You're so fucking unbelievably sexy. I can't wait to get you back to the apartment and peel off this beautiful dress. I've been thinking about what's under it all night."

I can't help but moan at his declaration. I want this dress off. This alcohol is making me hot. Again, maybe that's just Ryder.

Pulling up to the apartment, Ryder hands the guy some money. Maybe it's for his silence. I'd hate to get a bad review as a passenger.

Pulling off my heels, I basically run upstairs and open my door. "I have to use the restroom real fast. Don't move," I say to Ryder as I turn on my heels.

"Wait!" He exclaims. I stop where I am. Not bothering to turn around. He comes up behind me and slowly pulls down my dress.

It puddles on the floor. "I wanted to be the one to do that." Slapping my butt, he tells me to hurry up.

Running to the restroom, I pee, brush my hair, and pull it back into a braid. Opening the door to my bathroom, Ryder is already on my bed. And he is completely naked. Gone are the fancy clothes that surrounded him tonight, what's left is the raw, masculine Ryder. And God is it a work of art.

"Shit, you're even hotter with that braid in your hair."

I slowly walk over to him. I feel the atmosphere shift in the room. His raised browns turn into a hooded stare as I reach him. Touching my fingers to his ankle, I run my finger past his knee, up this thigh, and over his chest. His eyes turn red with desire.

"Sit on my face," Ryder demands. I'm shocked by his words at first, but the desire quickly takes over.

Unhooking my garter, I slide off my lace panties. Crawling onto the bed, I straddle him. I never take my eyes off him. In only my bra and thigh highs, I start to grind on his hardened length. If I keep doing this, he will slide right inside of me. I'm already soaked for him.

"I said, sit on my face. I want to taste you," He demands again. This time he isn't as nice about it. He grabs my hips and pulls me upwards as he slides down. I have to grab onto the headboard to keep from falling. The alcohol is still lingering.

He doesn't take his time. He doesn't tease me. He doesn't warn me. His tongue is on me in an instant. I'm not ready for the sensation he is giving me. I'm extremely sensitive as he works me over. His expert tongue works me up and down, back and forth until I'm grinding on him. I'm moving my hips where I want him. Selfishly taking what I need, I don't stop until I'm coming all over his face.

I roll off of him, completely spent. "I didn't say I was finished licking up my mess," he says as he climbs on top of me and slides on a condom.

His words, so vulgar, so dirty, turn me on even more. "I want you inside of me, now," I say, pulling on his hip, but he doesn't budge.

"That's not how you ask, baby."

"Please, I need you inside of me." Before I can finish my plea, he slams his hips forward. With a cry, I open my legs as far as possible. I want him as deep as he can go. He is a little bit longer than Logan, but he isn't as thick. I can't decide which feels better. They both know exactly how I like it. They both can read my body like pages in a book.

"Fuck, baby. You always feel so damn good. I can't get enough of this pussy," he cries out as he circles my clit with his thumb. His thrusts pick up pace, and I start to see stars.

"Turn over. I want to see your ass jiggle when I cum deep inside of you." Again, he isn't asking. He is telling me to. Scrambling to my hands and knees, I can't go fast enough.

He starts to slap his pelvis against my butt. "Do you want me to fuck you so hard, your toes curl?" Ryder growls into my ear as he wraps his hand around my braid. I moan in response because yes! Of course I want you to do that.

Pulling on my braid as he shoves himself so deep inside of me I scream. "Tell me what you want, baby. Use your words," he barks.

"Yes, I want you to make my toes curl. Please," I pant. I'm a complete mess right now. I would probably agree to do anything right now I'm so turned on.

With no reply, he does exactly that. Shoving my body down so he is flat on top of me, he grabs the headboard and pulls. He pulls over and over again as he thrusts into me. This new angle has my clit rubbing against the bedsheets, and I'm about to fall over the edge once again.

"I'm about to cum," he says as he slides his hand between my stomach and the bed. Rubbing my clit once, twice, three times, I cum with him. With a loud satisfying groan, he released into me.

"Damn it, baby. What are you doing to me? Usually I can last longer than that." Ryder laughs as he rolls over onto his side. Grabbing a tissue off the nightstand, he wraps his condom inside and shoots it into the trash can by my bed. "I could get used to that," I hear him say right before I drift off to sleep.

Waking up to Ryder kissing the side of my cheek, I smile. For a moment I think it's Logan. The way he brushes the hair off my back and kisses my shoulder reminds me of him.

"I have to go, baby. I need to get some work done." I moan at his talking. I may have a slight hangover, so his talking is aggravating me. "I'll text you later." I nod my head and go back to sleep.

When I wake back up, I look around. Thinking I'm going to find Logan in my apartment, but then quickly remember what happened last night. I can't help but feel sad. I had a great time with Ryder last night, but I will say the alcohol kept my feelings at bay.

I'm upset with him for leaving me last night, but I get it. Now that my mind is clear, I can think about what I really want. I don't want to make any rash decisions. I like Logan and Ryder both. They both show me a different side of myself.

It's too early to be having this kind of self realization. I need coffee and aspirin. Looking over at the clock, I'm shocked to see it's already 11:00 a.m. Wow, I must have been tired.

Thoughts of sex with Ryder flood my mind. The way he spoke to me, awakened something I never knew I enjoyed. This vulgar dirty talk was hot. Though sex with Ryder is anything but vanilla, I wonder if it's always like that? I'm sure there are times I will want to have more romantic sex.

Forcing myself to get out of bed, I try my best to start my day. I have zero plans other than to be as lazy as possible. I'm pretty sure I can manage it too. With this headache I'm nursing and these emotions I'm sorting through, I'm going to be the worst version of myself today. And I can't wait.

After showering, making coffee, and grabbing some food and water, I plop myself onto the couch. I don't plan on getting up from here until my bladder is about to explode. Instinctively, I want to text Logan. He would love a day of vegging out, but I stop myself. I guess I'll have to see how he acts with me tomorrow at work.

Before I start my movie, I call Becks back. I guess she tried to call last night. Is this about Logan? Did Logan tell Jarid about our fight? Or would you call that a breakup?

"You have some explaining to do!" Becks declares. Crap. I guess that's my answer. I'm sure Logan needed someone to talk to, I get it, but I can't believe Jarid told Becks.

"I can't believe you know. Wait, tell me what you know." Maybe he didn't tell her everything?

"I know it all, Alice Lilyona Mitchell," Becks scolds me. My middle name is Lily, but she likes to call me Lilyonna when I've done something wrong.

"Oh boy, here we go. It's not my fault he left. He spilled his feelings for me and then he walked out. What was I supposed to do?"

"He told you he LOVES you Alice. He didn't just say he wants to be with you. He told you he is in love with you and doesn't want to share you. That's pretty epic." I know Becks is right, but I'm just not ready to deal with this.

"I know. I just wasn't expecting it. Before I could register, he left. Then, I got upset that he left me there."

"At least he gave you money to get home. That's pretty nice to me. What guy does that?" Yeah, she may have a point there.

We go on talking about the rest of the story. I tell her about sex with Ryder, but she is so team Logan. Apparently there are teams now. Becks told Pixie about the situation. Of course she is team Ryder. I cannot believe this is happening.

"We're thinking about making shirts. You know, like the whole Twilight movie," Becks informs me.

"You better not. There are no teams. It's me needing to decide what I want to do."

I eventually convince her not to make t-shirts with *Team Logan* and *Team Ryder* on them, thankfully. I promise her I will come over tomorrow after work for some girl time. We hang up, and I start my movies.

Two movies later, I've only gotten up once to pee and refill my water. After the third movie, I walk over to the kitchen to find some food. Opening the fridge and fully expecting to find nothing, I see Logan's lasagna. It makes me miss him even more.

It's only been one day without seeing him, Alice. Get a grip.

Unable to help myself, I pull out my phone to text him. Closing it and opening it several times, I finally give in.

Alice: Look what I have.

I send him a picture of his leftover lasagna. He texts back right away.

Logan: Is that my lasagna?

I smile as soon as I see his text. How can you miss someone so quickly?

Alice: It is. Do you want it?

Logan: Are you bringing it to work tomorrow?

Alice: No, I'm hungry now.

Logan: You are going to eat MY lasagna?

He adds an emoji with a hand over the face's mouth.

Alice: You're welcome to come over and claim it for yourself.

Logan: I tried claiming it as myself. It didn't work out very well for me.

I wasn't expecting that message. He is usually funny and light hearted. He's never serious. Not until last night anyways.

Logan: Did you have a good time with Ryder last night?

Is he fishing? I don't want to tell him *yes, our sex was amazing too, but I did miss you.*

Alice: It would have been better had you stayed.

It's the truth without providing him with the entire truth. I just hope he doesn't press. Is it weird that I feel guilty for sleeping with Ryder without Logan?

Logan: I'm glad you had a good night, Alice.

I can't hear him talking, but I hear it in my mind. I hear the softness of his voice. I hear the tenderness, the longing, the caring as he speaks. It makes me sad to not have him here.

He sends a second text before I can respond, effectively ending our conversation.

Logan: I'll see you at work tomorrow. Enjoy the lasagna. Thanks for thinking of me.

Alice: I'm looking forward to seeing you.

I wait to see if he responds, but he doesn't. Tossing my phone onto the next couch cushion I groan in frustration.

I just want things to be like they were.

Chapter 22 Alice

My stomach is in knots as I make my way to my desk on Monday morning. After my eventful weekend, I'm eager to see Logan. I want things to go back to normal. Honestly, I don't want us to be just friends. I loved sneaking into the supply closet and having a moment with him. I love our banter. I love joking with him. He makes me smile constantly.

"Good morning, Mr. Miller," I greet him as he walks into his office.

"Good morning, Ms. Mitchell. Did you have a good weekend?" He asks as he pauses in front of his door.

"I did. Thank you. How was yours?" Do people actually want to know when they ask you about your weekend? I don't think they do, but even if he did there is no way I was going to tell him how my weekend actually went.

"Great. Glad to be back in the office," he says as he ducks inside his office.

You and me both.

I look over at Logan, but I can't see him.

"Oh, Alice. I forgot. I have a meeting at three today. Make sure I'm clear for the rest of the day." Mr. Miller pops his head out of his office.

"Yes, Sir. I'm on it," I say as I pull up his calendar. Thankfully, he doesn't have anything else scheduled, so I don't have to cancel anything.

Looking back over at Logan, I see him staring at me. My heart literally jumps and skips a beat. The corner of his mouth curls up into a half smile, and I stop breathing.

What is going on with me?

I want to go over there. I want to talk to him like we always do, but I'm not sure if he wants me to. We always have lunch together, I guess I can try to be patient until then.

⟫→

I CANNOT be patient until then. It's been two hours of me peeking at Logan. A few times I've caught him looking. Once, I was biting my pen as I was reading an email. Logan caught me, and I swear his eyes turned dark.

Was he turned on?

It has been a few days since we have slept together. Maybe he is horny, or maybe he wants me. I can't help but wonder if he went out last night and found someone to sleep with? My stomach twists at the thought, and I feel like I'm going to puke. I'm shocked by my jealousy. Is that what it is? Jealousy?

Is that how Logan feels when I'm with Ryder?

Just after 11:30 a.m., I can't take it anymore. Getting out of my seat, I walk over to Logan's cubical.

"Hey," I say as I reach him.

The moment he looks up, I feel my pulse start to raise. Has he always affected me this way? His pale green eyes search my eyes before he speaks. It's almost as if he is silently pleading with me. Is he in pain? Did I do that to him?

"Hey, Alice," he looks like my Logan, but he doesn't sound like my Logan. His voice is heavier. It's not that smooth joking voice I'm used to. He runs a hand through his glorious hair. How I want to be his fingers right now. I want to have his hands on me instead of on his own hair.

"You okay?" Logan snaps me out of my trance.

"Yes, I just missed the sound of your voice, so I was enjoying it." I give him a hopeful smile. Surprisingly he returns it.

"I've missed you too, Alice. You have no idea." The way he says this makes me nervous. Did he really miss me that much?

"Good. I'm glad to hear it. We still having lunch together like usual?"

"If you want to, we will," he says with a smile.

"I want to."

"So, how's Ryder doing?" He asks in a sarcastic way. Just as I'm about to answer, I realize I haven't spoken to him since Sunday morning when he left. I hope everything's okay.

"Fine," I say with a shrug. I really don't want to talk about Ryder if it's going to cause issues. He nods at me for a moment, deciding if he should continue.

"Okay, I'll meet you there in a bit. I have to finish some of these updates." He goes back to typing on his computer.

I pull out my phone as I head to the restroom.

Alice: Everything okay?

I don't get a response until I'm headed to the break room to meet Logan for lunch.

Ryder: Yes. Sorry I didn't text you yesterday. I got really caught up at work. It wasn't supposed to be that busy, but two assholes didn't show up for work. I ended up working until 8. Then, I had to do paperwork.

Ryder: I'll make it up to you, baby.

Alice: I'm glad you're okay. I was just worried for a bit.

Ryder: How is Logan?

I don't think Ryder cares if I spend time with Logan. I think he genuinely wants to know.

Alice: He seems a little distant and a little different, but I think we're working through it. We are about to have lunch together.

Ryder: Good. Enjoy your lunch.

Just as I put my phone down, I see Logan walking through the doors. A huge smile covers my face, and I can't believe how excited I am to have lunch with him. I was worried he was going to make up an excuse.

We eat lunch like usual. Talking about random things to get our minds off of the real issue we're having. Eventually, we will talk about it, but right now is not the time.

I tell him how I'm going to Beck's house after work for some girl time. I think that makes his shoulders relax a little more knowing I won't be spending my night with Ryder.

I could be spending it with you.

By the time lunch is over, I feel like we have gotten our groove back. Maybe he can come over tomorrow and we can really talk.

As we walk back to our desks, I grab his hand. The electricity that sparks between us is hazardous. I literally pull away in fear we may catch on fire.

Looking up at him, I know he felt it too. Has that always been there and I'm just now realizing it?

"Would you want to come over tomorrow after work? We can hangout and talk."

"Is Ryder busy?" Oh great. And we were doing so well.

"I didn't ask Ryder. I'm asking you," I cross my arms in the middle of the hallway. Thankfully, no one is around right now.

"I can't. I promised Jarid I'd be his wingman. Him and his girl broke up. He needs a distraction." The way he says it, it's as if he is talking about himself.

Is he going to the bar to hook up?

I don't like the thought. I also don't like how much it bothers me.

"Are you going to the bar we met at?" I'm not sure which answer I'm hoping for?

"Yes," he says as if it's no big deal. And maybe it isn't a big deal, but it punches me right in the gut.

"Okay. Maybe another time." I try not to let him see the pain in my eyes, so I turn to sit at my desk.

Logan and I haven't been around each other much today. Around 2:45 p.m., I see him walking over towards my desk.

He's finally coming to talk to me.

I smile up at him when he reaches my desk. "Mr. Miller said your keyboard has been sticking?" My disappointment is very visible on my face. He is coming over here for work, not to talk to me.

"Oh, yeah. It's not a big deal though. The M keeps sticking. You don't have to worry about it. This isn't really your job," I say with a laugh. I don't think the IT guy is supposed to fix the sticking keyboards.

"No, but replacing it is. I'm going to go grab you a new one," he says as he walks off. He returns five minutes later and hooks it up for me.

Just as he finishes installing it, I feel myself get light headed. The room goes in slow motion, and I'm pretty sure I'm about to pass out. "Alice," I hear someone say, but I'm not entirely sure who said it because I can only focus on the man standing in front of me, Noah.

Chapter 23 Logan

Alice isn't moving. It doesn't even look like she is breathing. Her face is white as copy paper, and her eyes have dilated. "Alice, sit down." I pull her down onto her chair and kneel in front of her. Grabbing the water bottle off her desk, I put it to her lips. "Drink."

Thankfully, she grabs it and chugs. Her eyes are fixed on something, but I'm not sure what. I haven't taken my eyes off of her. She seems to be coming back down to reality.

"Are you okay?" I ask again. Her color is finally starting to return. Her eyes find mine, and I start to smile.

"I-I'm okay," she shudders. I've never seen her like this. Turning to see what it was she had locked onto, I see a very well dressed man standing in front of her desk. Is this who she was having such a reaction to?

Dear Lord, please don't let her have another guy on the side. Damn it.

"Who are you?" I ask the man standing right by her desk. He is looking down on her as if he rules over her. I'm about to punch this guy in the freaking face if he doesn't stop.

"I'm Noah," he says as if I'm supposed to know who he is. I look at him with a questioning look hoping he will continue, but he doesn't.

"Okay, how can I help you?"

"I have a meeting with Miller," he says matter of factly. This guy is smug. He's probably a few years older than me, but he acts as if he is my elder. Like he expects me to dow down to him.

"You can go in," I hear Alice whisper from the chair.

"Alice, it was so good to see you. We should catch up," he says as he tips his head to her. What a prick.

So, he does know her. It sure as hell doesn't seem like she wants to catch up with him. That's for damn sure. And I won't be letting him come anywhere near her again.

"Who is that guy?" I ask, still kneeling in front of her. I rub the side of her face. It feels good to touch her again. To be there for her. To comfort her. I want to be that person for her. I want to be there when she needs me.

"He is from my old company. He is the boss's son." Okay, but that sure as hell didn't explain why she had such a bad reaction to him. Most people don't turn immobile at the site of an old colleague.

"What else, Alice. I know you're not telling me everything." Why doesn't she not feel comfortable sharing it with me? Are we already that far gone in our friendship?

"I don't want to," she bows her head.

"Is it that bad?" I'm starting to get worried. Did he harass her? Or worse?

"Love, you can tell me anything. I'm your safe place," I say as I tilt her head up to look at me. It's the first time I've used a pet name for her, and it feels right on her. She is my love.

She gives me a half smile as she throws her arms around my neck. Pulling me in for a tight hug, I let her. I let her because I've missed the feeling of her arms. Even though it's only been three days, it's been a long three days.

"It's okay, Love. Take your time." I rub her back in the most soothing way possible.

"I had a thing with him in the office," she finally says. That was not what I was expecting. Her words hit me harder than I was ready for. She had another office fling. Is that what I was? Just a replacement? I try not to react right away.

"When things went badly, I had to leave the company. My boss, Noah's father, was worried about a lawsuit, but I never even thought about doing that," She continues. Even her simply saying his name, it makes me angry.

"I left because I didn't want to have to deal with his drama. I didn't want to have to see him everyday." So pretty much exactly how she was with me. Is she going to leave the company now that she is done with me?

I feel my anger build up. "So office romance gone bad?" I ask knowing it has a double meaning. Her eyes go wide.

"It's nothing like what we have, Logan."

"It sure as hell seems to be a lot like what we had." I make sure to put the emphasis on *had* because what we *had* is over.

I feel hurt and lied to. "So you screw me and when that's not enough, you get Ryder to join in?" I ask a little louder than I meant for it to be. I'm not trying to get Alice in trouble, but I'm pissed as hell. And just as I do, I see Noah out of the corner of my eye.

Thankfully, Mr. Miller didn't follow him out here. "I came out here to see if you could grab us some coffee, but this is so much better." He starts to laugh.

"So you found yourself a new office guy to screw? That's rich." I'm staring daggers at this man, but he is only looking at Alice.

"Please, don't say anything, Noah. It's not like that," Alice pleads with the dipshit.

It's not like what? Meaningful? Special? I guess she's right. It's not like that. Just as I'm about to leave, Noah turns and faces me.

"I'm not sure why you all are fighting over her, it's not like her pussy is magical," Noah spits out. And all I see is red. Before I know what I'm doing, I rear back and punch Noah in the nose.

I hear Alice gasp and cover her mouth in shock. Noah stumbles but he doesn't fall to the ground. Mr. Miller comes out just as Noah advances at me. "That's enough. Get back in my office, Noah. Logan, I'll speak with you later," he says as he follows Noah back into his office.

"Logan, are you okay?" Alice grabs my hand that has blood on it. I can't even feel the pain from my hand. The only pain I feel is in my chest. The pain from Alice.

Pulling my hand away from her, I realize I have to get out of here.

Turning to leave, she grabs my shoulder. "Wait. Please, don't leave like this."

Turning to her, with all the pain evident in my face and voice. "I guess you weren't telling the truth when you said you hadn't experienced this kind of thing before. I mean, was I just a placeholder for you, Alice? Did I mean nothing? I guess that's why you were so excited to have Ryder?"

"No. That's not it, Logan. That's not it at all," she is pleading with me now, but I don't want to hear it. Especially not at work.

"Tell Mr. Miller I needed to take an hour of sick time. I have to go." I walk quickly back to my cubby where everyone is watching me. Great. That's just what I need, my personal business available for all my co-workers to witness.

"Logan," I hear Alice call my name as I grab my backpack. Turning back, I look at her for a moment. I sure as hell am going to miss this.

Chapter 24 Alice

Watching Logan walk out on me again while being so hurt was probably the hardest thing I've ever experienced. I didn't want to let him go, but it was not the time or the place to have that conversation.

"I cannot believe he knocked Noah out. Damn girl. Why didn't you record that shit? I would have loved to have seen his face after his nose got busted. Not so pretty now, are you?" Becks rambles on. I tell her everything that happened, and this is the part she is caught on. I'm pretty sure she could have a conversation with herself. She was definitely what I needed right now to lift my spirits.

"I literally cannot with you right now," I say to her as I give her a shove.

"But seriously, I can see where Logan is upset. I can also see where I would tell him that your past is none of his damn business. It could go either way. Depends on my mood that day." She gives me a smile.

"But what do I do?"

"Why are you so worried about it?" She looks at me 100% serious. I think for a moment. I wasn't really expecting her to pull such a 180.

"Because I don't want to lose Logan." It's really that simple.

"Okay, and you said you had forgotten that you hadn't heard from Ryder all day until lunch time?" I see her point before she even finishes her sentence. "It looks to me like you have already made your choice. You just aren't ready to accept it yet."

Is she right? Am I choosing Logan? Looking down at my phone I see my phone light up with a text. Holding my breath, I'm hoping Logan finally texted me back.

Ryder: How was the rest of your day, baby?"

I like Ryder a lot. He is so hot and he makes me try new things. He makes me feel amazing. I love being around him. So why did I get sad when I didn't see Logan's name on the screen?

Closing my phone, I look up at Becks. "Who was that?" She asks.

"Ryder."

"Why the long face then?" She tilts her head in a knowing manner.

"Because I'm worried about Logan," I say with an eye roll. I'm not ready to admit anything to myself yet because I'm not sure how I'm feeling. I don't want to jerk anybody around, so before I make my decision, I'm going to be sure.

"Let's talk about you for a minute. I'm tired of talking about my crazy life. How are you and Pixie?" I change the subject.

"Are you ever going to call her by her real name?" Everytime I call her Pixie, Becks rolls her eyes.

"I like calling her Pixie. It's cute."

"Well, Libby and I are doing great. We spent all day together yesterday. Maybe you should find yourself a girlfriend. I've said this before, chicks before dicks," she jokes.

"First off, I like dick way too much…that's my problem. Secondly, she does not seem like a Libby. Her name needs to be Pixie," I demand.

"You better not call her that to her face. If you piss her off…. Sorry. We can no longer be friends," She shakes her head. I know she's joking, but she keeps a straight face.

"I promise. Although, she may hate me for other reasons."

"We have already talked about it. She said if you and Ryder don't end up together, then we can all still be friends," Becks reassure me. I can't even believe how awkwards this will be. No matter who I choose, Becks is connected to them in some way.

"How did our conversation about you still come back to me somehow?"

"You're just so interesting. What can I say? Your life has turned into a reality TV show somehow," Becks says as she gets up.

She grabs herself a bottle of water and asks me if I want any. I nod my head and thank her.

"You know what I think?" She asks as she hands me the water.

"I'm sure you're about to tell me."

"You're very right about that. I think you need to take your ass home, and really think about it. Think about what you want. Don't think about what everyone else wants. Don't think about what's going to be better for everyone. Don't even think about what I want. You need to do what is best for you. Do what will make you happy, Alice." It's moments like these that truly makes me happy I worked at RedLights Co. If I hadn't, I never would have met her.

"You're right." That's all I say. Giving her a hug, I drive my confused ass home to sit and think about what I want.

⫸➔

Sitting at my desk on Tuesday morning, I close my eyes. I was up until midnight thinking, and I still haven't decided what the hell I want. Peering over towards Logan's desk, I still haven't seen him arrive. I don't see any of his stuff either.

Walking over towards his cubicle, I ask one of the other guys where he is. "Not sure. He isn't here."

Panic runs over me. Did they fire him for punching Noah? They can't do that. It was my fault. It was Noah's fault actually. He's the one that was incredibly inappropriate. Seeing Mr. Miller enter his office, I quickly march over to him. Knocking on his door, he waves me in.

"Did you fire Logan?" I ask Mr. Miller in a panic. He looks at me confused.

"No, I did not fire him, Ms. Mitchell. Why would you think that?" Relief washes over me. Thank God.

Then where is he?

He must see my confused look. "He took a personal day. Noah is a prick. I only took his meeting because his father asked me to. I'd never fire Logan over that jerk. Plus,

I'm sure Noah isn't going to be telling anyone that he got popped. His pride is way too big for that," Mr. Miller informs me.

I smile as I thank him and exit his office. Sitting down, I pick up my phone to text Logan. I notice I have a text from Ryder.

Ryder: Everything okay? I hope you're not ignoring me because I was busy Sunday.

Alice: Of course not. I've just been busy and a lot has been on my mind.

Ryder: I hope I'm one of those things.

Alice: You are.

Ryder: Good.

Pulling up Logan's texting thread, I send him a message.

Alice: I hope everything is okay. Mr. Miller told me you were taking a personal day. If it's about what happened yesterday, I'm sorry. I want to explain. I don't want us in this fight, Logan. You mean so much to me.

I wait for his reply, but it doesn't come. Closing my phone, I put it on my desk and finish my work for the day.

I'm horrible company today, even for myself. I'm in such a bad mood, I shouldn't be around people.

Beck's words run through my head over and over. *He told you he loves you. He is in love with you. I don't want to lose Logan. You said you had forgotten that you hadn't heard from Ryder all day.*

He loves you. He is in love with you.

My emotions hit me like a freight train. Why did it take me this long to see it? It's Logan. It's always been Logan. He's my best friend. He's the one I want to talk to about everything. He's the one I want by my side. He's the one that makes me laugh and puts a smile on my face. He's my yin to my yang, my peanuts to my butter.

I know I'm making the right decision. I want Logan. Not having him the whole day has been killing me. He is the one I want to tell all my news to. The good, the bad, the ugly, I know he will be there for me. This thing between us is just a misunderstanding. One I plan to fix tonight.

Chapter 25 Ryder

I have felt distance from Alice all day. It has me worried, but I'm trying to tell myself it's just nerves. She's fine. We're fine.

I spent all Monday playing catch up at work. Those two jerks that didn't show up for work, begged for their job back. Normally I'd tell them to go piss off, but I need guys. I'm tired of working these long days, so I put them on probation.

Today, I spent most of the morning buried in paperwork. Who knew being a foreman required so much paperwork.

"Yo, boss. There is a woman here to see you. She said you know her," one of my workers, whose name I have forgotten, informs me. My hopes shoot high. For a moment I hope it's Alice.

"Send her in," I say. As soon as the woman steps into my office, I regret inviting her in.

"Sandra, what the actual fuck are you doing here? At my work? Seriously?" I say to my deadbeat sister. I have one awesome sister, Libby, and one shitty sister, Sandra.

"I just wanted to come by and say hi. I heard you got a promotion at work. I wanted to say congratulations," she says as she darts her eyes everywhere by my face. I can see she is using again.

"It's been over two years since I got that promotion, Sandra. Why are you actually here?" I know why she's here. I'm just praying we can get through this as quickly and quietly as possible.

"Why are you always like that, little bro?" She is fourteen months older than I am, but she acts like she is fourteen years younger.

"Cut the shit," I say with zero amusement. I want her gone.

"Fine. Give me $100 and I'll leave you alone." She puts her hand on her hip as she waits for my answer.

"If you don't get your sorry, lying ass out of my office, I will call the cops and let them find whatever drugs you have on you."

"You wouldn't do that," she tests me.

Grabbing my phone, I start to dial.

"Shit, fine. I'll go. I'm glad to know you don't care about me anymore, little bro." She is trying to hurt me, but I've heard it time and time again.

"Just go. Get yourself some help, Sandra." I've offered her I don't know how many times to pay for rehab, but she won't go. I know one day, I'm going to get a call that she is dead. And I really am not looking forward to that day.

Libby was only nine when Sandra started using. She doesn't remember much about her.

Thankfully, Sandra leaves without a fight this time. Three years ago, she found my work site and made a huge scene. The foreman at the time had to call the cops. It was mortifying and heartbreaking at the same time.

I'm not sure why she keeps coming back around. I've told her the only money I'd be spending on her is the rehab.

Feeling my phone buzz, I see a text from Alice. My angry face is quickly replaced with a smile. She always has perfect timing. I know earlier today she had said she had a lot on her mind. I'm hoping she's feeling better today. I'm going to be pissed if Logan is giving her hell.

Alice: Hey, do you have time to talk?

Those words are never something you want to hear. I'm trying not to overreact though.

Ryder: I'll call you in a few.

I check my watch and it's just before 5:00 p.m. She must be just getting off work. I usually work until 6:00 or 7:00 p.m., but I may have to take off a little early today. God knows I deserve to cut out early after this crazy week I've had.

Alice: Of course. Just call me as soon as you can.

Her eagerness has me questioning her motives. What is so important? Unable to wait, I hit the call button.

"Hey," I hear her sweet voice, and it immediately makes me want to be inside of her. She just has that effect on me.

"Hello, baby. What's going on?" I hear her take a deep breath. This can't be good. I'm surprised to admit, she has me nervous.

"I'm sorry, Ryder... I just..." I cut her off before she can finish her sentence.

"You're choosing him, aren't you?" I can hear her sniffling.

"Yes, I'm sorry. I never meant to hurt you."

"Why? I thought we had something special?" I question. I'm the right choice for her. I know I am. I'm not going down without a fight.

"We did. I really enjoyed our time together. I loved us all together, but….I can't. I'm sorry," she sniffles again.

"The only reason you're doing this is because he is making you choose. If he never said he didn't want to share you, you wouldn't be ending things with me." I'm pissed off, but not at her. I'm pissed because I'm about to lose the most important thing in my life because some guy doesn't know how to deal with his feelings.

"Maybe so, but we are where we are. Please don't make this any harder than it already is. I feel horrible for hurting you," she says between sobs. She's crying now.

"Baby, stop crying. I know. I'm not upset with you. I just don't want to lose you," I admit to her. My head has dropped to the table, and I feel tears filling my eyes.

"Why are you being so nice to me? You should yell at me, call me names, something to make this easier. This is too difficult," she is crying so hard I can barely understand her.

"Let me come over. We can talk. I can't stand to hear you like this. I'm leaving work right now." I jump up from my desk and grab my keys. I'm determined to change her mind.

"No, Ryder. You can't. You can't come see me."

"Why the hell not, baby? Please. Let me come see you. Let me hold you one last time," my own tears are falling now.

If you had told me a few weeks ago that I'd be crying over a girl I just met…I'd tell you you were out of your damn mind. But here I am, crying over Alice.

No, we never got our time to really dig deep into our relationship, but we would have gotten there. She just needed to let us.

"If you come over, I'm afraid I won't be able to say no to you, Ryder. And I need to be able to say no to you." Her words physically hurt my heart. I've never felt like this before.

She needs me to let her go. Every bone in my body is yelling at me to fight for her. Every muscle in me is pulling me out of the door to get to her. The only thing that is keeping me here is her plea.

This is obviously difficult for her, and I don't want to be the one to make it even harder on her.

"I don't want to let you go, baby. But if that's what you need me to do, if that's what will make you happy, I will do it." I pull the phone away from my ear. I don't want her to hear me sniffling. I won't do anything to make things worse on her.

"Just remember, you deserve the very best. If you ever need me, you know where to find me." I try to reassure her.

Her crying has slowed now which makes my heart ache just a little less. "The gym," she says jokingly.

"Yes, baby. I'll always be at the gym, waiting for you."

"Oh don't tell me that. That will make me sad to picture you just sitting at the gym day in and day out." I can't help but laugh at her because obviously that's ridiculous. I hear her return my laugh and it's healing to my broken heart.

"But for real, Alice. If you ever need anything, I'm here," I say, trying to reassure her.

"Thank you, Ryder. I'm so very thankful I met you," she says and I can almost hear her smile.

"You too. Goodbye, Alice."

"Goodbye, Ryder."

Hanging up the phone, I can't help but feel like I'm letting the best thing in my life go.

Chapter 26 Alice

I can't stop crying as I sit in my car. I just got off the phone with Ryder, and I'm an absolute mess. I never wanted to hurt him. I never thought this is how we'd end when I met him at that bar.

I also never thought Logan and I would end up like this. My first assumption of Logan was wrong. After I got to know him, he was exactly what I wanted. I just pray it's not too late for us.

Wiping my tears from my eyes, I try to push my sadness for Ryder aside. Though I'm incredibly upset about Ryder, I'm hopeful for Logan and me. Looking down at my watch, I decide I should probably get out of my car and head upstairs.

I have to find Logan, and I know just where he is going to be tonight. Speeding up the stairs, I unlock my door as fast as possible. I need to eat something, shower, pick an unstoppable outfit that Logan can't say no to, and drive to the bar. And I have to do all of this in two hours. No problem.

Settling on my usual protein shake, I down it while I start the shower. As soon as it's warm enough, I take my time cleaning every inch of me. If my plan goes right, Logan will be exploring every inch of me when I'm finished with him.

Once my hair is laying perfectly flat, I walk to my closet to pick out the perfect outfit. I'm so antsy, I can't focus. Should I wear something casual? Maybe Logan would like something fancy? No, that would remind him of LaMoor's, and I don't want him thinking about that tonight.

Settling on my favorite skinny jeans that show off my plump backside, I pair it with a Red long sleeve crop top that will stand out in a crowd. Slipping on my black high heeled boots, I look myself over in the mirror. I put on a little extra make up in hopes to get Logan's attention.

Staring at myself in the mirror, I take a deep breath.
I can do this.

Logan and I belong together. I know it took me longer to realize it than it did for him, but I'm ready now. I want to give us a shot. I want to have him in my life as much more than just my friend. One thought keeps me staring at the mirror for a moment longer: is it too late?

Taking one more deep breath, I look down at my watch. It's 6:30 p.m. Becks told me they were going at 7:00 p.m. to have dinner at the bar. Becks was going to go with me, but Pixie had invited her to dinner for their one month anniversary. I can't really take her away from that. Then, she would be in the same boat as I am.

Grabbing my keys and my jacket, I drive over to the bar. As soon as I pull up, I spot Logans Audi. My stomach does so many flips I have to pause before I get out. I'm on the verge of throwing up that protein shake.

Get it together, Alice. You got this.

Making my way up to the double doors, I cautiously pull on the right one. I know this is what I want, but I'm terrified to spill my heart out and have him reject me. It's probably what I deserve. I mean, basically did the same thing at the restaurant. Then, I broke his heart yesterday at work. It wouldn't surprise me if he already had someone new. He was never hurting in the women department. The thought of that makes me want to puke.

If you keep thinking about that, you're going to shit your pants.

It's a fairly large bar, so it may take me a bit to find him. Going to the counter, I order a beer. At least I won't look so lost walking around if I have a drink in my hand.

As soon as the bartender hands it to me, he winks at me. "It's on me tonight, sugar."

I give him my nicest smile. "Thank you." Dressed in black jeans and a black logo t-shirt, it clings to his body in all the right ways. He's extremely cute, but he isn't the one I'm after. Making my way deeper into the bar, I spot an open high top by the pool tables.

Should I sit and wait for Logan to find me, or should I keep looking?

Just as I'm about to keep walking, I spot Logan in the back right corner. He has a blonde sitting on his lap as he drinks his beer. Jealousy rushes over me as I see her flirting with him. His eyes look disinterested, but his hand on her ass has me thinking otherwise.

I have no right to be upset with him. I had sex with Ryder just a few days ago. I don't feel like that was wrong, but I do feel bad about Logan not being there.

Taking a few steps closer to Logan, I lean against the high top table directly across from him and wait for him to notice me. It takes a whopping thirty seconds.

The moment his eyes meet mine, his mid laugh stops. I can't help but smile at the reaction he gives me. The hand that was wrapped around the blondes waist drops. He looks at me as if he feels guilty, but he hasn't done anything wrong. Although if that blonde doesn't get off his lap in 1.7 seconds, I'm going to rip the blonde right off of her.

He must see my plan for the blonde's future because he glides her off of him so fast, she nearly falls. I smile at the great decision he just made as he walks over to me.

I watch as he looks me up and down. Inch by inch, he drops his eyes. From my collarbone, to my boobs, down my legs, and back up. Be licks his lips when his eyes reach mine.

"What are you doing here, Alice?" He asks breathily.

His words may seem like he doesn't want me here, but his body is telling me otherwise.

"I'm here to take back what's mine," I say as I step closer to him. Running my hand down his chest, I grab his belt loop and pull him against me.

"Alice," he says as he places his hands on my hips to steady himself.

His close proximity has my body craving him. I want to grab him, kiss him and run my fingers through his hair. But I can't right now. I need to tell him how I feel. I need to explain everything and apologize.

Do I start with telling him how sorry I am about Ryder? Or should I be starting with my feelings for him? No, he won't hear anything I say until I explain things with Noah.

"Logan, I need you to listen to me. Okay?" I reluctantly move my hand that's in his belt looped to his hand. Thankfully he doesn't pull away.

"I think you've said just about everything." He looks over at his friend Jarid.

"Not even close. It's not what you think….I'm sorry….my feelings for you." I run all my thoughts together.

"Noah meant nothing to me. I haven't been ready for a real relationship, and he was just there. I ended it because he was a jerk, and I knew I deserved better. I left my job because he wouldn't leave me alone. He made my life hell there. It just wasn't worth it."

"Starting my new job and meeting the real you was the best thing I could have asked for. Which leads me to my next point." I grab his other hand so I'm holding onto both of them.

"I don't want to be your friend, Logan." I pause for dramatic effect. He rolls his eyes and it nearly makes me laugh.

"I want to be more than just your friend," I continue. "I want to be your best friend. I want to be the one that's always there for you. I want to be the one you share your exciting news with. I even want to be the one you tell your bad news to. I want to be there when you get that job promotion, or when you get passed over."

"I don't want to wake up another day without seeing your face or having a good morning text from you. You're my person, Logan, and I'm in love with you. I'm sorry for everything. Can you forgive me?" I plead with him.

Watching his eyes light up and his straight face turn into the biggest smile I've seen, I feel a sliver of hope.

"So you want me in your bed in the morning?" He asks, lifting his eyebrows. I slap his shoulder. Of course that's what he got out of that.

"You would say that." I roll my eyes.

"So, you love me huh?" He asks as he tucks my hair behind my ears.

"I am completely and hopelessly in love with you, Logan Spencer."

His smile takes over his beautiful face once again which causes me to smile. "And I'm hopelessly in love with you, Alice Mitchell."

"You know…I'm not sure I liked that woman all over you. I was about to walk over there and push her off of you. You better be glad you did it for me. I wouldn't have been as nice." I grab his t-shirt and pull him to me.

"I may have liked to have seen that cat fight. Want to go over there and tell her I'm your man?"

"You are my man, but no. I think I'll just show her," I say as I pull him hard against my lips. We don't move for a few seconds, but then I feel him slip his tongue inside of my mouth. The moment he does that, I forget where I am.

The room empties completely, and it's just the two of us left standing here. His hands move to the back of my head, deepening the kiss. My hands slide around him, pulling his chest to mine. When I do this, his pelvis conforms to mine causing a groan to release from my lips.

"It's been too long since I have felt you, Logan. I need you," I whisper against his lips.

"I'm about to take you right here on this pool table. I don't mind if they watch," he gestures to the crowd. "But I'll cut off their damn fingers if they try to touch you."

"I'm not sure why, but that was extremely hot. Say more things like that," I tease him.

He slaps my ass and my eyes go wide. Yeah, we need to leave right now, or I'm going to climb him like a tree. Grabbing his arm, I pull him towards the exit. I see him turn and wave to Jarid as I drag him.

I'm sure Becks will be getting the scoop tonight.

"Are you in a hurry, Love?" Logan chuckles from behind me. I'm still holding his hand as I drag him towards his car.

"You're damn right I am. Let's go to your place. It's closer," I say as I wait for him to unlock his car door, but he doesn't. Instead, he pushes me against the car and starts kissing me hard.

After two minutes, I have to pull away to catch my breath. I can feel my panties filling up. They are absolutely soaked. I've never wanted Logan as much as I want him now. I feel his length against me, and all I can think about is touching it. So, I do.

Grinding myself against him, I then reach down to cup him in my hand. To my pleasure, I earn myself a desperate moan. God, I want to give this man every part of me possible.

"Damn it, Alice. Get in the car." He opens my door and basically pushes me in. A laugh slips from my lips because he is just as turned on as I am. He's just as desperate. He's just as needy.

Chapter 27 Alice

Bursting through the door, we stumble into his apartment. I've only been here a few times, but I love it here. Usually we go to my place. It's closer to work.

Lifting me up into his arms, I wrap my legs around him. Feeling the heat between us, I feel excitement. It's like it's the first time for us.

Stumbling into the bedroom he throws me onto the bed. "Take off your clothes, slowly," he demands. I'm not sure what it is, but there is something different about Logan tonight. I must say, I don't hate it.

Pulling my crop top over my head, I drop it at his feet. Then, peeling my jeans off of me, I step out of them. Never taking my eyes off of him, I reach behind me to unbuckle my bra. I let it fall to the ground slowly.

His eyes drop to my heaving boobs. They are dying for him to touch them. Tucking my fingers into my panties, I slide them off of me.

Standing there naked in front of my man, I wait for his move. Licking his lips, he smiles down at me. Prowling towards me, still fully dressed, he admires me.

"Alice, I'm going to be rough with you tonight. I'm not upset with you, and I want you to know that I understand and forgive everything that has happened. But tonight, I need to be rough with you. I'll make love to you in the morning," he says as he grabs a handful of my hair and pulls on me.

I'm slammed into his lips as he pushes me onto the bed. We pull apart with a pop from our lips. My boobs bounce at the sudden movement, and I pant as I watch him remove his clothes.

Once he is completely naked, I scan his body. Taking it in, I memorize it as if I haven't seen it in decades.

"We're going to have to call Nasa because there is going to be a rocket launch tonight," Logan teases. It takes me a minute to understand what he is saying, but when I look down to see him touching himself, I get it.

"I can't wait to see that."

With a grin, he pulls me to the edge of the bed, slides a condom on, and looks up at me. "I'll be happy when we can be done with using these. I want to feel all of you," he whispers.

"I do too," I pant back.

"Soon. Are you ready, Love?" I nod my head and prepare myself, but there is no preparing one's self for Logan. Especially not the state he is in tonight.

He doesn't take his time. He is rough just as he promised. Pounding into me over and over, he is relentless.

Pulling one of my legs up, he pushes even further inside of me causing me to yelp.

"Fuck, I needed this." He leans his head back as he quickens his pace.

Rolling my clit with his thumb, he doesn't stop. He is keeping good on his word. He needs this, and I am more than happy to give it to him. I can be what he needs.

Sticking his thumb into his mouth, he sucks on it like a lollipop. "Your taste does things to me, Love," he says as he places it back on my clit and works me over.

I can feel my orgasm blossoming. I'm about to go over the edge, and I can't stop myself. With two more thrusts and two more passes of his thumb, I'm coming apart.

"I guess you did miss me," he says with a little laugh.

"I really did. Let's not be away from each other for that long again," I say, through heaving breaths.

He smiles as he slows his thrusts down. "Get up on the bed, with your ass up. This may hurt a little, but you will enjoy it." His words make me a little nervous, but I trust him completely.

Climbing up onto the bed, I do as he says. His demeanor has changed tonight. He seems to be desperate for me.

I feel him climb on top of the bed. I feel myself exposed to him, and I wiggle my ass to show him my need. Instead of him sliding inside of me, I feel him slap my ass. It makes me jump.

I wasn't expecting that.

Pain shoots through me, but as he rubs his hand over the sensitive area, the pain quickly turns into pleasure.

He does it again, and again. I'm writhing under his touch after the fifth one. "Logan," I cry. I need him so intensely right now. He was right, I did enjoy that.

"What's the matter, Love?" Logan asks as he rubs his dick against my opening.

"I need you, please." I'm desperate at this point, and I don't even care.

Putting his left hand on my upper back, he shoves me down further into the bed causing my ass to stick up even further.

Slamming inside of me, I let out a loud scream. Being this close with him is heaven. It's everything I need right now.

Grabbing my hair, he pulls as he slaps our bodies together. Leaning into him, he slides impossibly deeper. The feeling of the pleasure and the pain from my hair, sends me over the edge once more.

I hear a satisfying growl from his throat as he pumps once, twice, three times and comes deep inside of me.

Leaning down on top of me, we both catch our breaths. "Thank you, Love. I really needed that. I can't tell you how close to you I feel right now. I love you, Alice." Logan kisses me softly as he pulls out to discard the condom.

"I love you too, Logan." Pausing for a moment, "I have a serious question for you…" He gives me a nervous look. The last time we had a serious talk, I invited Ryder into our bed.

"What's that?" He raises his eyebrow.

"When are you going to be ready again? Because I want you in my mouth, from behind, and underneath me," I say as I reach my hand between us.

He is semi hard, but he's not ready yet. "You have to give me a bit, Love. But I can most definitely show my girl some attention until then. I've missed these lips," he says as he flips me around and pushes my legs wide open.

We stay like this for hours. It's a mixture of bodies, sweat, and love. Giving each other every last ounce of energy we have, we pass out in each other's arms.

I'm right where I'm supposed to be.

Epilogue - Alice

"Damn it to hell, Alice. I seriously still can't believe how good you feel," Logan says as he pulls out of me.

It's been two years since we started this whole thing, and we've had zero regrets. I moved in with Logan a year ago, and we have been going strong.

Waking up next to him every morning always starts my day off right. That is unless he wakes me up by snoring. Then, I'm usually not so happy. I've learned to deal with the ups and downs. It's like the roll of the ocean, it's impossible to always be going up. Eventually, you have to come down on occasion.

Any fight we have ever had isn't something worth us not being together. I know we are endgame, and I have a feeling a ring is in my near future.

I saw Logan outside of a jewelry store one day after work. He didn't know I went to the bookstore right across the street. I've been on edge since that day. It's been five, and I'm about to explode.

Work has been going great. Logan got an awesome promotion to head of IT. I wasn't sure what the difference was since he was already in charge of the other guys. He told me he is also in charge of the other location in Texas.

It does require him to travel some which makes me sad to be away from him, but our phone-sex game has gotten really good.

I'm still Mr. Miller's assistant, but he did promote me to *executive assistant*. It came with a decent pay raise which was nice as I don't have to do anything different.

"You ready for lunch, Love?" Logan comes up to my desk and kisses me on the forehead. We did have to disclose our relationship to HR, but they were good with it. We simply had to fill out a form.

"Yes, I'm starving!" I stand up and we make our way to the break room.

You'd think it would get annoying working and living with the same person. Being with them 24/7 should get tiring, right? Well it hasn't, and I don't expect it to. Of course, Logan has his moments where he jokes too much, and I want to throw a pillow at him. But I think that's pretty normal.

Cuddling in bed later that night, I look around our apartment and can't help but smile. I didn't know this is what I wanted, but I'm so glad I have it now.

Leaning over, I kiss Logan's naked chest. He really is a beautiful man, and he is all mine.

"I'd say everything we went through was worth it, wouldn't you, Love?" Logan asks with a smile.

"All's fair in love and war, right?" I ask, looking up at Logan's beautiful pale, green eyes.

"More like, all's fair in love and work."

Epilogue - Ryder

I've spent the last 6 months working my ass off at work and putting all my focus on it. It took me over a month to get over Alice. I'll say, it was the most difficult month of my life. I was an ass at work. No one wanted to be around me. Hell, I didn't even want to be around me.

I still see her from time to time when she decides to have a late workout. And every damn time she does, I think back to the time I fingered her on the treadmill. And every time I was reminded of that, I would have a set back.

I even thought about moving apartments, but I thought that was a bit dramatic. Thankfully, I was able to forget about Alice by sinking my dick into someone else. That always helps.

Now when I see her, I'm happy for her and Logan. Sure, I still think she is hot as fuck and she would be fun to screw, but she wasn't the one for me. I know that now.

Getting my usual late workout in, I spot that familiar blonde hair at the treadmill. And I curse under my breath.

Shit, not the treadmill. Anything but the treadmill.

I thought she had moved out already. I didn't think I'd have to relive this memory again. Do I ignore her? Do I go over and see her?

Just as I'm trying to decide, she turns to look at me. Those beautiful eyes light up, but they are not Alice's eyes! Those are….

What's her name again? Ainsley!

Looking her up and down, I smile as she smiles at me. Waving at her, I drop the weights and head over to her. "Well hello there stranger."

She smiles even more. "So you finally found me," she says as she slows her pace to a brisk walk.

"I've been searching . You must be playing hard to get," I wink at her. I must say I'm definitely glad I found her.

Unable to help myself, I scan her body up and down. She sees me, but she doesn't seem bothered by it.

"What are you going to do with me now that you've found me?"

This could definitely be an adventure.

ABOUT THE AUTHOR

Mom
Book Obsessed
TV Binger
Dog Lover
Foodie
Often lost in my other life that is writing…it's where the magic happens.

Learn more about Dahlia Dempsey and follow her on facebook for giveaways, teasers, and new releases. She will be releasing her first dark romance trilogy, and you don't want to miss it.
authordahliadempsey@gmail.com

Visit her website at:
dahliadempsey.com
Tiktok: @dahlia.dempsey.author
Instagram: @dahlia.dempsey.author

Other Books by Dahlia Dempsey

Our Time
💕 Romance
👤 Single Dad + Single Mom
🔥 Slow burn
📚 forced proximity
🌶 spice
🚫 Forbidden Love
😜 Reversed age gap

Love and Work
🐢 Rom Com
👯 Friends to Lovers
👨‍👨‍👧 Why Choose- at first
👫 Close Proximity
📚 Office Romance
🌶 SPICE spice baby
🌕 MFM

My Evil- Book 1
😈 Age Gap
❤️ He Falls First
🙊 Secrets
👫 Forced Proximity
🌶 Spice
💋 Opposite Attract
😱 Twist Ending

Special Thanks.

I want to thank all of my Beta and ARC readers. You all made this much easier for me.

To my beloved PA, Britney Oliver: You freaking ROCK! You are going to do great things.

To my author group: You all have given me so much support. I couldn't ask for more.

Last but not least: Thank you to Mandie DeVito for helping me edit my book. We all know how great I am with edits.

www.ingramcontent.com/pod-product-compliance
Lightning Source LLC
LaVergne TN
LVHW041747060526
838201LV00046B/938